Quantum Entangled

A Quantum Series Mystery

Douglas Phillips

In Greek mythology, the nine daughters of Zeus and Mnemosyne provided inspiration for human arts and sciences. Sometimes goddesses, sometimes water nymphs, these delightful women were known as muses, a name still found in modern words: museum, amuse, and music.

This story is dedicated to Marlene, my muse.

CONTENTS

1 TRAVELERS...1

2 PORTAL 11

3 WONDERLAND 23

4 BOT...33

5 MISSING 41

6 OUTSIDE...45

7 GIANT 51

8 COLONIST..63

9 ANCIENTS..75

10   BACKDOOR 85

11   REUNION..99

12   ENTANGLED 109

13   STARS 117

14   DISCOVERY 129

15   RHUBARB 139

16   COUNCIL..149

17   JOURNEY 159

18   WEDGE 171

19   HOMEWARD...183

AFTERWORD..197

ACKNOWLEDGMENTS 205

ABOUT THE AUTHOR 207

1   TRAVELERS

DANIEL RICE JOLTED upright in bed, his heart pounding and dangerous visions still swirling through his head. He blinked. Except for a LED on a heat exchanger, the room was dark. A drainpipe outside the bedroom window dripped in time with his heartbeat. Several deep breaths did little to settle nerves rattled by the recurring nightmare – only a fully awake, logically scientific mind could do that. And coffee.

Daniel slipped out of bed, taking care not to wake Nala. His stealth was unsuccessful. She lifted her head from the pillow. "You okay?"

He rounded the bed and sat beside her, pushing gently on her shoulders. "I'm fine, go back to sleep."

Physical coercion failed too. Her voice was groggy, but her concern showed through. "The desert island dream again?"

"Yeah."

She wrapped arms around him, her embrace calming his heart. Still newlyweds by most standards, they'd sealed the deal only six months before. The dreams, or visions – or whatever they were – had started not long after that.

When described as "the desert island dream", it didn't sound that bad, but dying of thirst was an agonizing way to go. No doubt just a dream, but repetition made it seem more.

Specific repetition.

Each time, he sat on hot sand slumped against a palm tree. Overhead, sunlight filtered through purple fronds. His parched throat ached as he watched a handful of sand slip between his fingers. Steps away, small waves on a turquoise sea lapped against a sandy shore. Colors seemed important, odd because Daniel rarely remembered colors from any other dream.

"I'll be okay," he told Nala and retrieved a glass of water from the bathroom. His throat always felt dry after the dream.

Cause or effect?

Strange how the brain works. Perhaps his subconscious was conjuring the same dream to alert him to a physical need for water. It was the best explanation he could come up with. But it didn't explain the other visions: a hooded figure, a soothing voice, an enormous disc of beveled glass floating in a sea of stars. Those dreams repeated too – short clips without any story behind them.

Daniel returned to bed, and Nala snuggled close. She put a hand on his heart. "Promise me you'll see that neurologist. Daniel, you've been places. You've seen things no one else has."

Daniel wrapped arms around her. "Yeah, maybe it's time."

It seemed to satisfy her, at least for that weird state of mind that exists at four in the morning. Once daylight arrived, he'd probably counter her concern by pointing out that he wasn't the only person who had jumped to the future. Three others had done it before him. Of course, one was dead, another was as crazy as they come and serving time in prison, and the third was Chloe Demers who had jumped only one day into the future during their tests at CERN. The Swiss government had put a temporary hold on all future time excursions until the astonishing science could be reconciled with the obvious need for careful management of humanity's future. The US government had agreed and had locked Daniel's time traveling belt in a vault.

Nala eventually fell asleep in Daniel's arms. For his part, the remainder of the night was time to think. He'd already seen one doctor and had received a referral to a neurologist specializing in sleep disorders. But more doctors were mainly for Nala's sake – that path didn't sound promising from Daniel's perspective. There was something else about these dreams, not easily described but felt deep inside. He hadn't put his finger on it yet.

Daniel managed to slide his arm from under his sleeping wife, and tiptoed downstairs. While coffee brewed, he pondered the unlikely events of his life. Chasing down missing astronauts. Meeting Nala at Fermilab and their efforts to decode an alien message. Extra dimensions of space. First contact with aliens. Crazy stuff. It had made Daniel famous.

He'd never wanted any of it. The White House job had been billed as a principal investigator for government science programs. Early on, the assignments had been routine. Finding the source of radon gas at a Nashville facility. Uncovering a vendor kickback scheme in Tulsa. Even the strange lights in the sky over Tonopah, Nevada had a perfectly ordinary explanation. No aliens involved.

Then came Core. And interdimensional portals. And time travel. Jumping thirty years into the future was the craziest of them all.

That was all in the past now. He'd given it up, cold turkey. No more visits with Core. No more celebrity life. Daniel and Nala had married, moved to Santa Fe, and started a new life with new jobs. Nala at Los Alamos National Laboratory and Daniel ending up as a science advisor for the New Mexico Department of Education. He still traveled regularly, but Santa Fe was now home, and Nala was the best reason to keep those business trips short.

Ordinary is fine by me.

Two cups of coffee later, sunlight peeked over the snow-capped Sangre de Cristo mountain range that graced their breakfast nook window, and Nala came down in a sleep shirt that hung to her knees. She wrapped slender brown arms around his neck and nuzzled close to his ear.

"Sunday. It is Sunday isn't it?"

Coded language. On most Sunday mornings, those silky legs of hers were wrapped around his back by now.

"I'll make it up to you later."

"Sorry, I didn't mean…"

"I know you didn't." He kissed her forehead. "Lots going on. How about some toast and coffee instead?"

"You've been analyzing. Desert islands, strange voices?"

He nodded. "Same old stuff. But I do have a new idea."

"Shoot."

"Honestly, a neurologist won't help much. My case is too…"

"Fucked up?"

"Unusual. I've literally been swallowed by a moon-sized cybernetic organism, for example."

"And I'm glad Core didn't digest you. I still don't trust that thing. But I get your point. You're not the average patient. You've been around."

"Right. A neurologist doesn't have the knowledge base to provide the right diagnosis. But… I could talk to Zin."

"Doctor Zin?"

"Well, maybe not a doctor, but he's well connected. He's got full access to every bit of knowledge in our galaxy, something humans don't have."

It was true. Humans had not yet gained full membership into Sagittarius Novus, the consortium of civilizations scattered across the galaxy, or been given access to the galactic encyclopedia, An Sath. While efforts were underway to complete humanity's membership, rumors had spread that it wasn't going well.

Nala set her coffee down and lowered her voice in a humorous impersonation of Daniel. "So, Zin, I'm getting these funny dreams about a hooded man, broken glass floating in space, and dying of thirst. Got any alien pharmaceuticals for that?"

"*Beveled* glass, not broken. Get your mocking points down."

"Beveled. I stand corrected. But what's Zin going to do for you that a neurologist can't?"

"No idea, but…" He was hesitant to tell all. She wouldn't laugh, but he hated to burden her. "Look, it's more than repetitive dreams. It's a feeling. Coming from… some other level of reality."

She locked eyes with him and raised a brow. Her expression wasn't disbelief – they'd both seen other realities firsthand. She was waiting, ready to hear whatever he had to say. And Daniel was finally ready to tell.

"It's like something out there is calling me."

This time she spoke with no hint of mocking. "Coming from a scientist, that doesn't sound good. You never told me this part. Fess up, Daniel. All the way."

"Nothing more to tell. It's a feeling, that's all. I don't know what it is."

"A feeling that something is calling you."

"Or maybe some*one*. Could be a person. I'm hearing a woman's voice in one of the dreams. Might be her."

She drank the rest of her coffee in one gulp and stood up. "Come on, let's go."

"Go where?"

"The airport."

Nala had a history of spontaneity, but Daniel was still taken aback.

"I, uh…"

"Pack a bag, scientist. We're going to Geneva."

He finally got her point. Nala absorbed new information quickly and could flip mental frames as fast as most people changed their shoes. "Zin's not in Geneva. Last I heard he was in Beijing working with the Chinese."

"Then we're going to Beijing. Right now. And don't say it can't be done. You've got the government connections." When Daniel stalled for a millisecond, she pulled on his chair. "Daniel, don't make me kick your ass."

He stood up, towering over her by nearly a foot. Petite in stature, but Nala's determination could be fierce. Daniel held up hands in surrender. "You're right. I'll go."

"*We'll* go."

"Alright, we'll both go."

He laughed at the absurdity of flying to China on a moment's notice. "I hear Beijing is lovely in December. Below zero cold. Killer smog. We'll get a cinderblock hotel room overlooking the open-air sewage plant."

She rolled her eyes. They'd both been to Beijing before. Stereotypes only fooled the uninformed.

****

They checked into the five-star Eclat Hotel, walking distance to the Temple of the Sun and only a quick taxi ride to the Imperial Palace. From the outside, the hotel was a glass version of Space Mountain at Disneyworld, towering into the sky with twin peaks sharper than the Matterhorn. On the inside, blades of glass magically attached to a curving metal framework, polished to perfection. The ultra-modern look was complemented by delicate flowering trees and ancient Chinese statuary that made the oversized lobby look more like an art museum.

Still in a time-zone daze, they were guided to a spacious room overlooking a city crowded with tall buildings, colorful temples, and rectangular parks. Zin, now famous across China and regularly mobbed by curious citizens, had agreed to meet them at the hotel for afternoon tea – after they'd had a chance to rest.

Nala stood at the floor to ceiling window staring out at the bustling city below. "It's not that cold, maybe we can get out to some of the temples while we're here."

"I'd love to." Daniel came up from behind and wrapped arms around her. "Right after we pay a visit to the Higgs Factory."

The Chinese particle accelerator was smashing all records for energetic collisions. They'd recently confirmed the existence of the long-theorized graviton, a discovery that had not only earned Chinese physicists the Nobel prize, but launched the country into a new era of scientific cooperation. China had done well in its program of self-rehabilitation.

Nala smiled. "Neutrinos and gravitons. You sure know how to sweet talk a girl."

He pulled her close and whispered into her ear. "I do. Now, about that Sunday play time we missed."

Nala laughed. "It's Monday here. International Date Line and all that."

"Doesn't apply. Our bodies are still on New Mexico time."

He lifted her off the ground and she fought back – fake, but surprisingly strong – squealing and laughing until tangled arms and legs collapsed onto the bed.

Two hours later, they were happy, rested, and presentable, sitting together at a quiet table in the corner of the hotel's tearoom. Black tea. Quite good.

A flurry of activity and raised voices from the hotel lobby gave the first clues, and seconds later Zin swept in with an entourage of Chinese hangers-on trailing behind. He wore a traditional Chinese Tang suit with knots down the front and dragon themed embroidery that wrapped around each side. The alien android had never looked better.

"Dr. Rice, Dr. Pasquier," he said, bowing Chinese style.

Daniel and Nala stood. Conversation from other tearoom guests turned to whispers. Stolen glances were mostly directed at the famous android, not the American couple graced by celebrity presence.

"Zin, you've acclimated well to China," Daniel said.

"I do love it here. The people are kind." He motioned to his entourage who took seats at a nearby table, then pulled out the chair next to Nala. "Have you been to the Higgs Factory yet, Dr. Pasquier?"

"Funny, Daniel and I were just talking about that. I'm game, but first things first."

"And second things second," Zin replied, then cocked his head. "Sorry, is that an expression?"

"Not really." Nala stifled a laugh then put a hand over Zin's metallic fingers and squeezed. It was only the second time the two had met – Daniel and Nala's wedding being the first – but Nala's relationships with people she liked went from zero to a hundred in the first five minutes. Zin had been no exception.

"Then Dr. Rice's business first." Zin's flat metal eyes flicked left then right. "How can I help?"

With his table companions hanging on his every word, and the Chinese conversations elsewhere in the tearoom returning to normal, Daniel related his story. He provided the technical details of the recurring dreams, and, after Nala's encouragement, the emotional details too.

"Is the repetition increasing in frequency?" Zin asked.

"Maybe. Probably. I guess I should be tracking it on a chart."

Zin furrowed his unibrow as effectively as any human in distress. "If it were anyone else, I would suggest consulting a doctor. But since you are a time traveler…"

He put a hand to his chin and closed his eyes. There was little reason for the android to pause in thought – he was probably communicating.

"He's got something," Nala said.

Zin's eyes flicked open. "It's only a possibility, mind you."

"But?"

They both waited. Pulling information from Zin wasn't the most straightforward approach, but he had proven himself reliable once answers were delivered.

"Entanglement," Zin said with authority.

"Elaborate, please," Daniel said.

"Timeline entanglement. Rare among randomly chosen individuals, but more common among time travelers like yourself. Formally referred to as entanglement of conscious experience across multiple probability pathways in a multiverse. At least, that's what the Litian-nolos will tell you. They are the experts in this dysfunction, not me."

"Is it like quantum entanglement?" Nala asked.

"In a way, yes. Two particles, once entangled…"

"Remain entangled even when separated by great distance," Nala finished.

"Or across timelines," Zin added.

Daniel stepped into the physics. "But you called it a dysfunction. How does quantum entanglement affect a macro-scale object like me?"

"Far more difficult to predict since humans are new to timeline manipulation. The Litian-nolos would know more but establishing a relationship with a time mentor could be tricky."

Time mentor. A term Zin had mentioned to Daniel last year in Geneva just before Daniel's thirty-year jump to the future. Litian-nolos were known to be time manipulators, and they'd had some successes in guiding their species toward a better future. But Zin hadn't said anything about establishing a relationship with them. As far as Daniel knew, humans had never met Litian-nolos. Maybe it was time they did.

"Why would it be tricky?"

Zin's puzzled look made it clear the answer should be obvious. "Because humans are not yet members of Sagittarius Novus. While I have high hopes that the Council of Equivalence will vote in your favor, none of us can be sure. Until then, the only way for humans and Litian-nolos to interact would be at Jheean."

Nala's eyes lit up. "Alien interaction. I like it. Are Litian-nolos friendly?"

"Quite friendly," Zin replied. "In their way."

"Let's go then, we're free. Took a week off from work."

Daniel was slightly less sure than his spontaneous wife. When Zin mentioned places with unfamiliar names, they might be anywhere in the galaxy. "So, how would we get to Jheean?"

"Easily," Zin answered. "We won't even need to leave China. Part of my work here has been to create a second portal."

2   PORTAL

THE SECOND FLASH of yellow light was just as bright as the first.

Daniel blinked hard. A hood covered his face blocking any view. Fuzziness made it feel as if he'd been napping and suddenly jolted back to consciousness. Something in his memory was missing, like a name misplaced and never quite recalled. The odd feeling would pass, but he'd just lost several minutes of reality that he'd never get back. Jumping more than a thousand light-years across the galaxy could do that.

The hood retracted. He lay on an interdimensional transfer seat – essentially a fancier version of a hair stylist's chair, though Chinese versions were decorated with beautiful calligraphy. CNSA, the Chinese National Space Administration, had also provided the travelers with auto-adjusting thermal jackets. Helpful, given the distinct chill in the Jheean air.

They had transported to a curved glass enclosure bathed in orange light. An equally transparent horizontal platform spanned its midsection. In one direction, an orange sunrise washed out the view, but overhead stars winked in a black sky.

Daniel unbuckled and slid from his seat. Nala, already up, stared beyond the glass enclosure, her mouth agape. Their transparent perch floated high above a magnificent desert planet that stretched to a gently curving horizon in the distance. Puffy clouds floated far below casting shadows across the browns and rust-reds of a dry landscape.

Daniel pivoted in a full circle to absorb the beauty of their lofty vantage point. A blue-green ocean dominated in one direction. In another, mountains tinged in purple towered above the desert floor. "Miles and miles," he whispered. If the intent of this entry point was to impress, their hosts had done well.

"I've been to the observation deck at the Hancock building in Chicago, but this…" Nala never finished her sentence.

Far below, a flower-shaped structure with six petals stretched across the rusted landscape nearly halfway to the horizon. Each petal narrowed as they joined their counterparts at a six-sided hub in the center. As Zin had explained, the word *jheean* meant hexagon in some alien language – its meaning now plainly clear.

Across the six-petal flower's roof, a complexity of surface detail – boxes, ovals, and lines – gave some feeling for distance. Not any ordinary building, this sprawling megastructure was easily the size of a small city.

Daniel took trepid steps across the transparent platform. Solid enough, even if the inner ear was staggered by the unsettling view down. Their transfer seats stood on pedestals in a slot, no different than their departure point. The new CNSA Transport Hub was a sprawling technology center only ten minutes away from Beijing by bullet train. At the far end of the enclosure, a white portal doorway revealed nothing but a starry sky through its opening. China – and everything else that represented Earth – was now very far away.

The horizontal platform joined a curving glass wall with silver ribs spaced every few feet to create the cocoon-shaped enclosure. The whole thing perched atop a clear tube – ten or twelve feet in diameter – that thinned to a thread in its plunge to the planet's surface. It was as if someone had balanced a fishbowl on a plastic straw. Like it or not, they were the fish. The tube was no doubt sturdier than it looked. Not only was it the only thing holding them up at these stratospheric heights, but it might also be their only path to the surface.

Daniel scanned the neighboring petal of the six-sided flower and detected a second glass enclosure, hovering above it. A similar thread connected to the surface. There were others, too, each petal conforming to the same pattern, though the tiny cocoons at the far side of the hexagon only revealed their presence from faint glints of sunlight.

Dramatic six-way symmetry, but for what purpose?

Twenty-three species, he answered to his own question. Every member of Sagittarius Novus would need an entry point with a suitable environment. Zin had hinted as much. Four species per petal was one possibility, but unlikely. Daniel imagined that requirements for life might assume a bell curve like any other random distribution, and from probability theory human requirements for oxygen, temperature and pressure likely fell somewhere in the middle. Of course, there would be extremes too. This cocoon held an atmosphere that could represent a mountaintop on Earth – fifteen degrees Celsius with pressure set to eight hundred millibars, according to Zin – but other cocoons might be far more exotic.

Nala slipped an arm around Daniel's waist, her eyes never leaving the remarkable view before them. "I'm going to write a travel guide when we get home. Top ten sights in the Milky Way. Jheean is definitely on the list."

"I wonder how we get down?"

"Open the hatch and jump into the slide?" She pointed to an almost indiscernible circular outline on the platform floor.

"I'm game," Daniel lied with a grin.

"I've done some pretty hairy waterpark slides." Her eyes scanned the tube's full length, several miles, at least. "Well, maybe not this tall."

Daniel peered through the platform's clear floor, examining the connection point of the cocoon to the tube. "Maybe it's not a slide, maybe it's just a pedestal?"

"Or a stem," Nala answered. "The rest of it *does* look like a flower."

Daniel nodded. "Maybe this cocoon will decouple somehow and fly down to the surface."

"No wings."

"Braking thrusters, then."

"Where's the propellant stored?"

Daniel shrugged. He rapped knuckles on thick glass, sounding a dull ring. It was certainly a glorious perch, but also a holding cell with a single exit to the surface.

With a crackle of electricity, the portal doorway flashed opaque, and Zin stepped through as if on a Sunday walk.

"I see you're enjoying the view." Zin said, strutting the length of the platform like a showman on stage. He'd changed clothes, now wearing a silver body suit that really wasn't much different than his metallic skin. "Welcome to Jheean. Or more properly, Jheean e' Bektash, the enclosed hexagon city of the desert planet Bektash. A planet your own astronomers discovered, I might add."

"Really?" Nala asked. "But aren't we a thousand light years from home?"

"One thousand eighty-four," Zin corrected. "Human astronomers labeled this planet Kepler-508b."

"Ah, yes, our exoplanet surveys," Daniel said. "Gliese, Kepler, TESS. We catalogued quite a few planets back in the day."

"Before we discovered spatial compression, which made it all moot," Nala added.

"Perhaps moot now, but your science for the past several hundred years has been exceptionally good." Zin's positive view of humans had never faltered in any conversation Daniel could remember. "And now it's time to enjoy the fruits of your labor. You have arrived."

Zin spread his arms across the glorious scene at their feet. "Jheean is quite a remarkable place, as you will soon see. While you're here, I'm confident the s-bots will ensure your comfort."

"S-bots?" Nala asked.

Zin pointed outside. "S-bots are Jheean helpers, in a way. Here comes one now."

Daniel squinted. Zin probably had better vision than a hawk on a utility pole. A tiny dot moved upward from the depths of the tube. Within seconds, the glint rose past the tube's midpoint revealing an elongated ovoid the color of gold. It reminded Daniel of one of those gelatin capsules used for fish oil supplements.

The capsule-vehicle rocketed straight up, then slowed as it approached the platform, coming to rest just below them. Its smooth shell resembled gold foil and might have been no thicker.

"Classy transportation, Zin," Daniel said. "Nala and I thought we might be jumping straight into the tube."

"You could, of course," Zin said with no hint of sarcasm. "With graviton active cushioning you'd be perfectly safe, though unguided descent is more an emergency procedure – or for those in a hurry."

Daniel choked on his laugh. "Don't worry, Zin, we'll take the approved transportation."

Nala looked miffed at the missed opportunity to ride the Death Slide, but with the golden capsule now docked they'd ride to the city in style.

With a hiss, the circular outline on the floor popped up like a manhole cover. It slid to one side, and several glass steps unfolded to create a stairway into their transportation.

A mechanical grasshopper the size of a dog hopped up the steps, then stood erect on its hindquarters at the platform's edge. Its body was covered by a layered shell – khaki in color – giving an appearance of overlapping roof tiles. An elongated head perched on top with bulging black eyes. Forepaws and thick legs that folded back at a knee joint completed the grasshopper appearance.

Right behind, a man climbed the steps. With thinning white hair framing a deeply wrinkled face, he looked out of place though Daniel was sure he'd seen him before.

The man reached out. "Nikolaus Jensen, UN Secretary General."

Nala shook his hand first, then Daniel. "Ah, yes. Our ambassador to Sagittarius Novus?"

"Ambassador implies membership. Negotiator is closer to the truth." Secretary Jensen, a former prime minister of Norway, had been selected as the head of a small team of diplomats in humanity's quest for membership in the galactic consortium. His dour expression seemed to match the news reports of little progress.

The mechanical grasshopper who reached only to Jensen's beltline twitched, then issued shrill pitches like a piccolo played by a spiteful musician. Zin nodded thoughtfully, then squealed his own tune in return. The irritating exchange continued for a few seconds. Nala covered her ears.

When they were done, Zin explained. "I'm afraid it's bad news. This s-bot tells me your entry has been declined."

Jensen nodded. "I wish the news were better. I spoke to the Litian-nolo delegation and approved your visit to Jheean myself. Apparently, someone overruled me. I'm afraid I don't have much sway here yet. Even this little fellow outranks me."

The s-bot twitched left and right, its black glassy eyes seeming to survey the two new humans that were barging into its domain.

"Do you suspect the Toraks?" Zin asked.

Daniel had heard the name. One of the original five members of Sagittarius Novus, Toraks were said to be obstinate people who followed rules based on pride more than logic. But if they were the primary voice arguing against human membership, those details hadn't been part of any public news report.

"Honestly, I don't know," Jensen answered. "Yes, the Toraks have been problematic but only in a general sense. I have no idea why they'd object to Dr. Rice and Dr. Pasquier specifically. There may be more that we don't understand."

"Ask him," Daniel suggested, nodding toward the bot still standing ramrod straight on its haunches.

"I did," Zin responded. "I didn't get an answer and really didn't expect one. S-bots have limited intelligence and would not normally be entrusted with important details. The bots are used for hospitality purposes but also for security. This bot accompanies Secretary Jensen to enforce the restriction. I suggest we do as it asks."

Daniel surveyed the small creature. If it had a weapon, it was well hidden. Those thick hind legs looked powerful though, perhaps less like a grasshopper and more a wallaby.

Zin continued. "I will go to the surface with Secretary Jensen. Perhaps I can find out what went wrong. You could wait here, but it might be more comfortable if you simply return to Earth. Press the recall buttons on your transfer seats and you'll be back at the CNSA hub in seconds."

"Disappointing," Daniel said. Nala agreed with a vigorous nod. If their trip to Jheean turned out to be a dead end, it was probably back to conventional doctors – or live with whatever disturbance was roiling inside of him.

The s-bot produced a sharp squeal, and Secretary Jensen started down the glass stairway. As Zin passed, he wrapped both arms around Daniel in an awkward hug.

"I'm so sorry Dr. Rice," Zin said as if consoling a bereaved relative at a funeral.

The android pulled away, leaving Daniel astonished at the unusual show of emotion. It wasn't like Zin at all, which meant something else was going on. He made no other irrational moves, instead following Secretary Jensen down the short stairway and into the gold capsule.

The s-bot twitched its head a few times as if assessing compliance of the remaining humans, then hopped down the stairs. The cover slid back into place, sealing the platform once more. A few seconds later, the capsule dropped away, rapidly accelerating as it descended to the flower-shaped structure far below.

"Well, that sucks," Nala said.

"It does." Daniel put his hands on his hips, feeling something out of place in the small of his back. He reached behind to his beltline, grabbing metal tabs sticking out from his pants. Turning to Nala, he held two blue aluminum wafers in his hand. Each was about the size of his thumb but coin thickness. There was writing on one side – unintelligible.

"What are they?" she whispered, taking one of the wafers.

"I don't know, but I think Zin stuffed them under my belt when he hugged me."

A light went on in Nala's eyes. "Sneaky little devil, that Zin. I'll bet they're access cards."

"You think Zin wants us to follow? To the surface?"

"He did act rather strangely. Should we?"

"Can we?"

Nala shrugged. "Why not? According to Zin, this tube uses graviton active cushioning."

"Super cool physics term, but is that really a thing?"

"Sure, well... theoretically. We talked about it at Los Alamos, now that we know gravitons exist. The idea is to align the graviton-quark interactions along a chosen vector – like iron filings in a magnetic field. It could produce a local gravity adjustment to reduce or cancel the natural gravitational pull. Maybe these people figured it out."

Daniel studied the floor, the transparent cover now flush with the platform. Even if they could open it, a long tube dropped precipitously for miles. He turned the wafer in his palm – a key, no doubt, but they would need to find the lock. Studying the surroundings, he noticed a flat metal pad sticking out from one of the silver ribs, the only extension in an otherwise smooth enclosure. Waving the wafer over the pad, the cover lifted and slid away, lowering glass steps that now ended in midair.

"Nice," Nala said, dropping to hands and knees at the edge of the precipice. Daniel joined her, peering into the hole. A slight breeze came up from its depths. Cool, breathable air, the same as in the cocoon. The tube continued straight down until its gentle arc obscured the remainder of its enormous length.

Daniel gulped. "That's a long way down."

Nala waggled her eyebrows. "You should know by now, Daniel, that distance is meaningless in the quantum world." She pulled a hairclip from her ponytail and dropped it into the hole. It fell, as any object formed from quarks would. "We can do this. Graviton cushioning would need to be built into the structure itself, not the capsule. It's why Zin said we could jump and be perfectly safe."

"In an emergency, as I recall."

"Or if you're in a hurry." Nala grinned.

She stuffed the blue wafer in a pocket and started down the stairs, grabbing a rail on one side. The breeze blew her hair straight up as she descended.

"I don't know about this." Daniel squatted at the edge of the precipice. "Even if you're right about the physics and we survive, what happens when we get to the bottom? Zin didn't seem to think it was a good idea to piss off s-bots. There might be an army of them down there."

"He gave us two security cards. Surely that means we can go wherever they went, right? Come on, you're a science investigator. So... investigate."

Daniel swallowed. "Most of my projects don't start with a five-mile leap."

Nala took another step, glancing down into the abyss just below her feet, then up to Daniel. She smiled slyly. "Why did you marry me?"

A non sequitur, but he'd come to expect that from Nala. "Um, because I kind of like you?"

"Try again."

"Because you're spontaneous?"

"Closer. You say you want a simpler life, but that's a lie. You're not a government bureaucrat, a clock-puncher, a stay at home and do crossword puzzles kind of guy. Nope, you're Daniel Rice, scientific adventurer. You figure out stuff nobody else can. You go places nobody else goes. You take chances. And *that's* why you married me."

She took another step. "Well, here's another adventure, just beginning. An alien city is down there. Answers are down there. Answers that we both need."

She lifted one foot from the bottom step and dangled it in the air. "Last one to the bottom buys the margaritas." Nala leaped off the stairway and dropped into the tube, her arms flailing.

Daniel hurried down the steps just as Nala disappeared around the curve of the tube. "Crap! What was I thinking when I married this lunatic?"

Daniel took a deep breath. Then another. He closed his eyes, gritted his teeth, and stepped off the stairway to an instant rush of wind.

3   WONDERLAND

DANIEL HAD TO ADMIT that Nala's critiques were sometimes spot on. After all, he had skied some of the steepest runs at Val d'Isère. Bivouacked overnight dangling from a few pitons hammered into a sheer granite face. Bailed out of a perfectly good airplane strapped to a professional jump guide. Adventures of the vertical kind. And each had been thrilling in its own way.

But this plunge was closer to insanity.

A gale dragged the thermal jacket to his armpits. Cloth flapped wildly in his face. The blast blew up his pants legs, chilling body parts normally kept warm. Extending legs and arms flattened his body horizontally and slowed the heart-in-throat plunge. If there was any gravitational cushioning within this Death Slide, it hadn't kicked in yet.

Daniel blinked away tears, squinting against the atmospheric onslaught. The planet's surface was still far below, visible through the transparent sides of the tube. A gentle curve ahead reduced his inside view to a quarter mile, possibly less. Nala was nowhere to be seen. If they somehow survived, a frank discussion about the wisdom of spontaneous decisions was overdue. Possibly marriage-ending.

Of course, a splat would end the marriage even quicker.

At least the wind wasn't getting any stronger. Either he'd achieved terminal velocity or Nala had been right – the tube itself was controlling his rate of descent. Regardless, the cold became difficult to ignore. He dragged the thermal jacket down across his chest, feeling its heating elements kick in.

Outside, the ground rushed upward. *Pull the ripcord*, he imagined his jump guide would be telling him – more likely, screaming. With no parachute handy, an unzipped jacket might produce an incremental decrease in velocity, but a splat still awaited.

The tube straightened slightly. Still no signs of Nala ahead. No matter. They were both committed to Zin's declaration that the slide wouldn't kill them. This plunge would end soon, one way or another.

Seconds ticked by. Flapping clothes quieted – only a little, but noticeably. He pulled his arms in and yet his velocity still slowed. The roaring wind eventually reduced to a gentle breeze, calm enough to allow him to curl into a seated position – minus the chair.

"What do you know, gravitational control."

Nala was right. Daniel twisted backwards, a motion easier than he expected, like floating in a swimming pool. Far above, the glass cocoon stood out like a glinting diamond against a deep blue sky. The stars were gone now, washed out in sunlight that illuminated a thick atmosphere.

His descent slowed to elevator speed with the destination not far ahead, a glass dome near the tip of one petal of this six-sided megastructure. Barren desert lay on either side of the petal.

Seconds later, Daniel passed through an opening in the dome and floated gently into a circular chamber beneath. To one side, two gold foil capsules stood side by side. At the chamber's front, a curving pane of glass walled off a hallway that stretched into the distance.

Like Superman, Daniel drifted down to a marble surface, alighting gently on his feet. Nala was nowhere to be seen, either inside the glass chamber or outside in the adjoining hallway. Daniel tucked in his shirt and straightened his thermal jacket while surveying the surroundings.

The hallway outside the clear glass was at least fifty meters wide and equally tall. Empty for the first few hundred meters, it widened toward what looked like a village, fully enclosed, and complete with bustling residents. Figures of varying sizes and shapes intermingled among buildings small and large, with some structures climbing the hallway walls like overhanging balconies. Murmurs of voices were unmistakable. A community, no doubt, but so far none of the residents had noticed his arrival.

No sign of Nala in the chamber or the hallway. No evidence of trauma. Certainly, no splat; she must have touched down as gently as he did. But then what?

Her hairclip.

She'd dropped it as a test, but the clip wasn't anywhere on the floor. No gutters at the edge, no drainage holes for it to fall into. She'd picked it up. There was no other explanation.

Hairclips don't just disappear, but people don't walk through solid glass.

Daniel rapped knuckles on the glass wall, producing a dull ring no different than the cocoon enclosure at the top of the tube. Solid. No way out in that direction.

He stepped over to the two gold capsules that magically hovered a foot off the marble surface. Open doors revealed seats inside. He'd have transportation back to the cocoon, but that wasn't the direction he was heading. At least, not yet.

Next to the capsules, a circular outline recessed into the wall exactly matched the capsule's cross section. Another manhole cover, this one horizontal. If he could find the corresponding security pad, it might be a way out. He still clutched the blue aluminum wafer in his hand.

Daniel circled the room twice inspecting every edge and surface. Nothing. "Who builds a landing chamber with no way out?"

Clearly Nala had figured it out, though why she hadn't waited for him was beyond comprehension. He'd been less than a minute behind her.

Daniel tapped the wafer to one of the capsules. No response. He waved it in the air. Still nothing. But when he tapped it against the glass wall, a seam appeared where only solid glass had been a second before. The seam quickly enlarged to a triangular doorway with cool air flowing in from the hallway.

The voices were louder now, mixed with clanks, whirrs, and the occasional whistle. Not your typical human village but then Jheean had been billed as a galactic meeting place. According to Zin, Sagittarius Novus members came here from home planets hundreds, even thousands of light years away. Sort of a United Nations Building for the Milky Way.

Even if they hadn't noticed him yet, his entrance would be obvious. Except for a series of translucent glass panels set at regular intervals, the hallway led to only one place. No overhangs, no cubbies. No shadows to hide in. There'd be plenty of eyes on him. Nala might already be there.

Daniel stuck the security wafer in his breast pocket like a badge that proved he was authorized to be here. The s-bots might not agree, but he started walking anyway. A bounce in his step verified a gravity slightly lower than Earth.

As he passed a glass panel, Daniel peered inside. Its smoky translucence prevented a clear view but as he withdrew, an amber glow flashed beneath his foot. The glow blinked three times, outlining an oval that elongated and climbed partway up the wall. It didn't seem threatening, more like an attention-getter. Daniel tapped a toe on the light, and it flickered in response.

Communication?

The light remained steady. Daniel stepped on it. His fingers touched the portion that climbed the wall. The light flashed three more times then surged forward, dragging him with it. Off balance, he quickly righted and found himself sliding down the hallway on nothing but a glowing oval of light.

Personal transportation, with speed easily controlled by exerting a slight pressure against the wall. There was little sensation of touching, as if a frictionless buffer had extended beneath the oval. Within a minute, he'd progressed most of the hallway, with the village buildings looming ahead.

The hallway widened into a circular chamber beneath another dome. Two-story buildings with open windows on top were fronted by an open-air market where a bewildering variety of creatures congregated. Skinny stick figures shuffled through narrow gaps between market stalls that featured exotic alien wares. Squat birdlike figures perched on nearby benches. Savory smells wafted through the air mixed with unfamiliar voices.

Daniel released his hand from the wall, and the light oval slowed to a stop. He stepped away and scanned the incredible scene.

A garbage can on wheels flew by. Its hard-plastic exterior implied automation but flexible limbs on either side gave a hint of biology inside. An oversized centipede scurried through the crowded plaza on dozens of feet. At its leading end, a helmeted head twisted toward Daniel, staring from behind a dark visor.

There was no point in hiding. Every sensory organ in the village was glued to the newest visitor to Jheean. Nervous, Daniel threaded his way through the market alive with strange beings, voices, clicks, and vibrations, along with smells both fragrant and pungent. In one stall, a slab of charred meat turned on a rotisserie. At another, dozens of glass jars filled with red liquid were stacked into a pyramid. The hairy form behind the counter motioned to its wares by way of extendable floppy ears.

Daniel stopped. "Hello." Not exactly the most profound thing to say on first contact, but the encounter felt the same as when traveling in a foreign country. Fear of miscommunication kept most people mute.

The hairy shopkeeper snorted through a miniature version of an elephant's trunk.

"Sorry to bother you, but I'm trying to find someone. She looks like me, but with longer hair like yours." Gestures accompanied his words but were just as ineffective.

The shopkeeper stared blankly, then lifted a jar with one ear.

Daniel waived. "Yeah, no thanks. Maybe I'll check with someone else." He continued walking, scanning the crowd of shapes. Nothing remotely human anywhere to be found.

A fence blocked his path. A living fence, moving, vibrating, but a fence nonetheless, complete with fence posts and rails. He stopped, watching with a perverse interest as thousands upon thousands of tiny gnats forming the structure fluttered their silvery wings in unison. Then, like a marching band on a football field, the gnats dissolved their fence and reformed into a six-foot tall clamshell. The motion of their tiny wings produced a shimmer across the shell's surface almost like they were making a statement about the mollusk's shape.

It's a Szitzojoot.

Zin had mentioned Szitzojoots in a press conference as an example of one of the more exotic species humans could encounter. With no clear definition of an individual, Szitzojoots were regarded as a composite species, or hive.

His forward access blocked, Daniel crossed his arms and watched the astonishing performance. The hive reformed into a humanoid shape, complete with humanlike arms that crossed its chest, mimicking Daniel's own pose.

"Fascinating," Daniel said aloud. A buzz came back from the collection of gnats sounding very much like an echo, though fuzzier.

"You can speak?" Daniel asked.

"*Zhoo ken zpeek?*" The hive buzzed back.

The hive probably had no comprehension of the English words, but the integration required to produce a single voice was astonishing. As if to prove they were more than mimics, the gnats quickly reformed into a tight collection of balls, six balls shaded silver via upturned wings, six shaded black, and six much smaller balls that orbited around the central collection.

"*Zhee zha bosh,*" the hive buzzed.

Daniel smiled. They'd formed a carbon atom, possibly making a statement of the creature's chemistry. Though utterly different in physiology, the Szitzojoot had not only demonstrated intelligence, but apparently shared the same molecular basis as humans. Perhaps we weren't so different after all. Humans were nothing more than a vast integration of individual cells, communicating with each other via complex chemistry.

Daniel could watch the show all day, but he was on a mission. "I'm looking for my partner." He held up two index fingers side-by-side, pointed one at himself, then sent the other finger off on an imagined trek. His gestures were improving.

The hive buzzed into the shape of a hooked cane, wrapped the curving portion around his back, and nudged Daniel into the direction of the hook's point. The pressure on his back was light, but noticeable.

"She went this way?"

The hive buzzed in unison. Whether it had understood his gestured question might require years of study by the best linguists. For now, Daniel took it as a good sign that he might yet find Nala. He thanked the helpful hive and set off in the pointed direction. A vast corridor stretched into the distance, even wider than the first.

With twenty-three species in this consortium, Daniel wondered what other beings might still be ahead. No doubt the most exotic would be found within other petals of the Jheean flower structure, but as an air breather Daniel might never meet them.

At the corridor's edge, another light oval patiently blinked. If the cocoon's view from above was any indication, the central hexagon might be located at the far end of this grand avenue. Unfortunately, there was no way to know if Zin or Nala had ended up there. So far, the natives had been friendly enough, but limited communication lowered his chances of success. He scanned the market once more, even studying each of the open upper-story windows. No sign of Nala.

Why didn't you wait for me?

Worry produced instant tension. Worry not for himself – he'd be fine – but something had happened to her. Without any better plan, Daniel forged ahead. He stepped on to the blinking light oval. A touch to the wall whisked him away, this time without the clumsy off-balance start.

Now a city-sized avenue, Daniel passed several intersections with crossing hallways where various species intermingled. The light oval simply passed through each intersection continuing in a straight line. If there was a way to turn left or right, he hadn't figured that part out yet. Assorted beings zipped in the opposite direction along the far wall. Apparently, Jheean traffic kept left, English style.

Well ahead, a small grasshopper figure made great leaps toward him. Daniel's pulse quickened at the sight of the s-bot. He hopped off the light oval even before it slid to a stop. The bot was now only a hundred meters away and closing the gap quickly.

A narrow side passage was the only hiding place, and Daniel ducked down it. It wasn't much of a passageway, requiring a sideways shimmy, but that limitation might be to his advantage.

The passage narrowed further, and its ceiling lowered. Down at ankle height, a row of translucent panes decorated the wall, like the panes he'd passed in the first hallway but one-tenth the size. Next to one small window, a miniature oval of light blinked, barely big enough to transport a mouse. Daniel suddenly felt like a giant.

Like a policeman's whistle, a shrill pitch sounded behind. With progress ahead virtually impossible for a human-sized behemoth, Daniel turned to face his pursuer.

The s-bot blocked the passageway's entrance. Its large glassy eyes stared straight ahead. Rising high on its hind legs, the metallic grasshopper squealed an ear-splitting wail that could easily have shattered glass.

In the same shrill tone, it voiced a single word, "Human."

4   BOT

FOREPAWS ENDED IN sharp claws. Dull black eyes were fixed on Daniel like potential prey. Any attempt to overpower the bot would be a poor option, perhaps deadly. Negotiation was a better approach, particularly if this security bot could speak English.

Daniel shuffled toward the entrance of the passageway and held up the blue access wafer. "I'm authorized." He hoped lasers weren't about to spring from some orifice.

The mechanical grasshopper made no move to step aside. Overlapping plates shimmered like chrome body armor. Up close, its lifeless eyes showed no sign of intelligence behind them.

Daniel tried once more. "Do you speak English?"

The creature twitched its head to the left, then straight. "Able. Limited." Its voice was clear enough, if pitched near the upper limit of human hearing.

"I'm Daniel Rice, a human *pre*-authorized to meet with the Litian-nolo delegation." It was an honest statement, even if the Jheean security database had been more recently updated to include two human intruders. Daniel imagined a *Most Wanted* poster with his and Nala's photographs prominently displayed. Perhaps they'd already captured her. The thought made his heart sink but strengthened his resolve.

"Daniel Rice," the s-bot repeated, then said the name once more as if comparing to the poster. It issued several shrill tones and a few clicks. Its dark eyes receded, and its head flipped forward at a hinge on its neck, presenting the top of its metallic skull. Waves of light danced across the shiny metal and a very different voice emerged. Deeply resonant. A voice that vibrated, like a musician's bow pulled across the strings of a cello.

"*Daniel Rice*," the voice reverberated.

Daniel pinched his brow. "Core?"

"*In a form, yes.*"

Since first contact, Daniel had spoken to the gatekeeper several times, once in person – if being transferred *inside* the moon-sized cybernetic organism counted as in-person contact. The voice was the same varying pitch, the same buzzing sound, but more distant than previous contacts. "You're speaking through this security bot?"

"*Yes. And you have entered Jheean*," Core responded.

"I have," Daniel said. Plain speaking was the best approach with an all-powerful entity like Core. No excuses, no pleas, no whining. Just straight talk. But no mention of Nala in case they didn't know.

The vibrational voice emanated from somewhere on the s-bot's body, but the creature never moved, keeping its head hinged open.

"*Your access has been denied.*"

"So, I've heard. Why?"

"*The Council of Equivalence intervened.*"

Daniel was familiar with the name though the inner workings of the governing body for Sagittarius Novus were obscure. Without full-fledged membership, Nikolaus Jensen was humanity's only representative to the council and by his own admission, Jensen didn't have much pull.

"Why intervene? What have I done?"

"*That is a council matter. This bot will escort you out. Do not attempt further evasion, the bot is armed.*"

Daniel clenched his jaw. He'd confronted Core once before in his effort to get answers for the implosion at Fermilab that had nearly cost Nala her life. Then, as now, getting information from the gatekeeper was like pulling teeth.

But this joust wasn't over yet. Core had never been concerned with the trivial affairs of humans – who lives or who dies – but the cybernetic entity had responded to bigger-picture topics. Daniel elevated his pitch.

"When vital information is withheld, humans are at a disadvantage. It's not fair, and it's not in anyone else's interest either. My goal today is simple. I seek only to communicate with the Litian-nolo delegation. But our representative, Secretary Jensen, regularly receives the same confrontational stance from some members of the council. Three years ago, as I recall, you invited us to join. Are you withdrawing that invitation? Or is there something else we should understand?"

Even reasonable questions might be flirting at the edge of skirmish. There was no telling what commands Core might issue to the s-bot, or what "armed" might imply. Even Zin had been jittery about confrontation. For that matter, Zin might be chained to a dungeon wall right now for his subterfuge in this little adventure.

Core spoke with authority. *"Humans can be dangerous."*

The accusation wasn't new, but maybe this time it had risen to the ranks of representatives with voting power. "Maybe so, but dangerous primarily to ourselves. I doubt we could ruffle any feathers among the members."

"Daniel Rice, you underestimate human recklessness. I have learned much about your species since our first contact."

"That may be true too," Daniel admitted. "But I also know our strengths."

"As do I."

A stalemate. Not bad, considering the power of the opposition. Core could have thrown him out without another word. For that matter, Core could probably turn Earth into a blackened cinder with a snap of its cybernetic fingers. The fact that there had been no such threat in three years spoke volumes. Core might be cagey, the council might be fickle, but this collection of galactic civilizations and their gatekeeper had shown no hostility toward humans.

Daniel took a deep breath, pushing his luck. "I admit humans are complex but we're a whole lot better than dangerous. You know that as well as anyone. Three years ago, you rescued our astronauts and set us on a path to membership. We accept the responsibility to prove our value to the council. But give us that chance. We can't do much sparring if we're thrown out of the arena."

There was a pause as lights flashed across the s-bot's skull. "*Standby.*" A minute later, Core came back. "*There is no more I can do. Exit now, Daniel Rice.*"

"But what about…"

"*Exit now.*"

The s-bot clicked, and its head returned to an upright position. Eyes protruded, resuming its grasshopper appearance. It screeched, "Ahead. Follow."

So much for having contacts in high places. He'd gotten some intelligence that might be useful to Secretary Jensen or others back home, but any meet and greet with the Litian-nolos was fading fast. For now, returning to Beijing might be the best option.

But Nala is still here… somewhere.

He had no theory as to why she hadn't waited for him back at the tube's landing zone but there was no way to contact her unless he gave her name away to the s-bot. Deep within a zone of alien technology, his mobile phone was nothing more than a camera.

The s-bot hopped forward, and Daniel grudgingly followed. They reentered the main avenue heading back toward the village that Daniel had just left. At the next intersection, the bot stopped. Its head twitched to the left and twitched again. "Urp," it belched.

"What's wrong?" Daniel asked.

The bot paused like it was listening for something, then turned to the right. "This way."

Daniel shrugged and followed. The passageway was smaller and became darker as they walked. It finally reached a dead end in front of another of the ubiquitous glass panels, this one glowing in translucent light.

"Something we need to do before we leave?"

The bot faced Daniel, its uniform black eyes giving no hint of purpose. Without warning a blue-white light shot from a gap on the grasshopper's head, enveloping Daniel in an electric arc head to foot. An electric sting touched his neck, shoulders, and hips. The shock wasn't severe, but instantly uncomfortable.

"Uhh!" Daniel winced as the intensity increased. With crackling snaps and pops, he was lifted from the ground inside a ball of electric arcs.

"Stop it! I'm not resisting!"

The glass panel slid open to reveal a metal chute angled almost straight down. The electric field dissolved as quickly as it had formed, and Daniel dropped into the chute. He plunged down a slide, frantically grasping at metal walls too slick for any traction.

Flailing, he smashed through a hinged door and into bright light. Hot air shocked his senses.

Daniel fell for another ten feet, thumping to solid ground. The crash knocked the wind out of him. He rolled across a sandy surface gasping for air, panicked that outside air might not even exist. Blue sky and a brilliant sun overhead confirmed his predicament.

His diaphragm recovered, and he instinctively sucked a lungful of whatever this planet might harbor. Carbon dioxide, ammonia, cyanide. It could be anything, but no amount of logic could prevent an inhale when the body demanded it.

It's breathable.

Daniel got to his knees and sucked in another breath of hot air, grateful for the satisfying feeling of oxygen filling his lungs. Scattered desert plants and a few tumbleweeds confirmed a possible oxygen source.

He got to his feet, squinting in bright sunshine. Sweat beaded across his forehead. Easily fifty degrees Celsius, maybe higher. The air was thick, and while several more breaths confirmed the life-preserving oxygen, there was no way to know what other constituents might be invading his body right now.

What the hell did I do to deserve this?

The s-bot's action made no sense. Certainly, this wasn't what Core meant by an escort to the building's exit.

He stood at the base of a vertical wall of metal that stretched indefinitely in both directions. No windows, no openings. Its full height was impossible to tell, but it began to curve away about thirty meters overhead. There would be glass domes up there somewhere, but they weren't visible from his position.

A few bleached bones of some unidentified animal were scattered across the sand, and a tattered half-buried cloth flapped in the hot breeze.

Well above, the hinged door he'd smashed through was now resealed. If he had a ladder and a crowbar, he might stand a chance of prying it open.

With a loud bang, the door flew open, ejecting a mass of flailing mechanical limbs. Daniel ducked as the s-bot smashed to the sand and rolled several times. It shook its head, hopped upright, and surveyed the surrounding desert.

The s-bot's head twisted up to the hinged door, now closed once more, and it shrieked with a single high pitch. Paused, then shrieked again.

On the third mechanical shriek, Daniel finally yelled, "Stop!"

The bot went silent, its head still twitching. Daniel kept his distance. "Aren't you the guy who just threw me out? What are you doing out here?"

"Not protocol," the s-bot answered. The thing made no moves toward or away from Daniel. It just sat in the sand looking like a lost puppy.

"What, somebody threw you out too?"

"Not protocol," the bot repeated. It seemed confused.

"Well, I'm glad being dumped in the desert isn't protocol. I'd hate to think this is standard practice." He glanced up to the blistering sun. "Know of any doors we can use to get back in?"

The bot just stared ahead. Its voice softened to a pathetic whine. "Not protocol."

Daniel shook his head. "Doors. Portals. Hatches. Anything like that?"

The bot stared, silent. Deflated.

"You do understand it's at least fifty degrees Celsius out here."

"Sixty-four point seven," the bot corrected.

"Fabulous. A hundred-fifty-degrees Fahrenheit. I don't know about you, but unless I find a way back in – and soon – I'm toast." The sun beat down mercilessly. The hot breeze made it even worse. Daniel moved closer to the building where a sliver of shade covered a miniscule portion of his body.

"Why did you throw me out anyway?"

"Not authorized."

"Yeah, right. So, what was wrong with taking me for a ride on the gold capsule back up to the portal?"

"Disposal required."

"Disposal? Core told you to dispose of me?" There must have been some misunderstanding. Core had never been vindictive. Or a liar.

"Not Core."

Daniel cocked his head. "Somebody else?" It was possible another player was involved. The bot had certainly behaved strangely in the main corridor.

"Security override. Protocol 19."

"You got an override command, but not from Core?"

"Not Core," the bot stated again.

"Then whoever is giving the orders, fooled you. They wanted me gone, but you were evidence of my conversation with Core. So they dumped you too."

"Not protocol."

"I couldn't agree more."

The bot lowered to the sand gurgling a series of urps and acks like it was gagging on something. Daniel surveyed the desert landscape. Knee-high dunes were interspersed with rocky ground where desiccated plants grew. Heat waves shimmered at the base of a distant mountain range.

Daniel wiped the sweat from his brow, already wishing he had a bottle of water. "No question, we're dealing with something bigger than we thought."

Visions filled Daniel's head. Recollections of dreams where he was dying of thirst.

5   MISSING

NALA STEPPED OUT of the gold capsule, double checking to be sure this was the correct petal in the six-sided flower of Jheean. "Well, that didn't work out so well."

The glass-enclosed chamber appeared to be the same place where she'd touched down fifteen minutes ago, but Daniel was nowhere to be seen. She wasn't really expecting him to be standing around.

Her plunge through the tube had been no issue, but she'd alighted on the arrival platform a bit too soon. Zin, Jensen, and the security bot were still in the hallway outside. Avoiding the bot's attention, she'd grabbed her hair clip and jumped inside one of the gold capsules hovering at one side.

At the time it had seemed like a good hiding place, but the door had closed automatically, and the capsule zipped through a circular opening on the wall. She'd searched for controls. No brake pedal. Shouting commands made no difference. She'd tapped her blue security wafer on anything and everything, but the capsule continued down a long tunnel.

It had popped out at another landing area, similar to the first but filled with clear water. Drowning seemed a distinct possibility. The capsule slowed but thankfully the door remained closed. After a brief pause, the capsule continued into another tunnel. The next petal was filled with an orange cloud, not something she had any interest in breathing. Three more landing areas passed, including one where the cold was so intense drips of water clinging to the capsule's exterior crackled and popped as they froze.

At the sixth petal, the circuit of Jheean was complete. A tap on the door with her wafer had done the trick, depositing her back where she'd started – minus Daniel. She knew her spouse well enough to be sure he'd jumped behind her. Since he wasn't anywhere to be seen, he'd either taken his own tour of the petals, or was somewhere down the hallway.

Hallway, for sure.

There was no sign of Daniel beyond the glass but activity further down the hallway held promise. Buildings. People. Maybe a whole village. She tapped her wafer. Not surprisingly, a seam opened.

They do glass pretty well here.

Voices coming from the village made it clear she was within reach of help. It had only been a small delay. Fifteen minutes, no more. Certainly, Daniel would be among those voices. He'd be waiting for her. He'd probably already located the Litian-nolos, found a friendly bar, and ordered a round of margaritas.

Or was analyzing some alien you-are-here map. That'd be more like Daniel.

She'd pay good money to have a working mobile phone right now. A twenty-first century woman without the essential tools of twenty-first century life. It was an odd feeling.

Nala ran toward the voices and buildings. It looked like one of those cute Mediterranean villages, though entirely indoors. Alien, of course, not that it mattered. Someone would have information. She might even find the person they were supposed to meet, though recognition could be an issue. She didn't have a name. For that matter, she didn't even know what a Litian-nolo looked like.

Nala slowed as she entered an alien community alive with activity. In the center of an open-air market, five stick creatures at least ten feet in height stood in a circle. Their narrow limbs shimmered with tiny spines that stuck out at right angles like the cholla cactus found in Arizona. Each held a silver cup that it tipped with regular frequency to an opening in the middle of a narrow head. Another pointy appendage quivered in synchronization with twitches of its head, making a buzzing sound as the appendage tip made complex motions in the air.

Virgons?

NASA katanauts had visited their planet just last year, a team that included Daniel's old partner, Marie Kendrick. There had been plenty of photos, and the vibrational gestures of their language had become a staple of YouTube videos though few humans could claim more than passing familiarity of the simplest words. Even the Virgon label was a misnomer. Human fingers couldn't manage the complex gesture representing their actual name.

The group of stick-cacti people paused in their vibrational drinking ritual as Nala approached. They looked bigger in person. Each creature twisted at its midsection to observe the newcomer. Nala pasted a broad smile across her face and mentally thumbed through a selection of social greetings that might apply. None did.

Wish I'd paid more attention to those videos.

Nala waved. One of the stick figures twitched, vibrating its speaking appendage in a small circle like the human finger twirl for *speed it up* but more likely meaning something else.

Greetings earthling? Or get the fuck out of my town?

The group re-formed into a line, and each member stored their silver cups into a cloth band wrapped around their midsection. In unison, they held one appendage to the sides of their thin heads and then dropped it back down – a greeting of some sort.

Nala walked to within a few feet of their line. Eyes bulged. Antennas wiggled. Up close, they looked a lot like praying mantises.

An insect that eats its mate.

Thousands of sharp needles covering their appendages did nothing to improve her gut reaction, but a pleasant woody scent wafting from the aliens matched their sticklike appearance.

Sure, they're giant bugs but they smell nice.

43

Smile still in place, Nala touched the side of her head and twirled a finger. "Hello… ladies and gentlemen or… um, other. I wonder, have you seen someone like me pass this way?"

She pressed a palm to her chest, instantly thinking she'd touched the wrong part of her body since Daniel didn't have breasts, but just as quickly realizing that stick aliens covered with needles probably wouldn't notice the difference.

One creature stepped forward holding out a prickly appendage. There wouldn't be any handshakes with this species, though it appeared that touching wasn't its goal. Flaps of thin skin fluttered over bulging eyes. It twitched its narrow head to one side twice, then pointed to a hallway on the opposite side of the domed gathering area. The tip of its appendage vibrated rapidly enough to make a slight buzzing sound in the air.

Nala smiled sweetly. "So kind of you. I'm not from around here. You can probably tell."

The cactus stick people stood silent, staring. There were no further vibrations.

"Great! Well… um, it was nice to meet you. Maybe Daniel and I will see you around sometime."

She bowed and withdrew. The prickly mantises touched the sides of their heads once more.

Not bad. But harder than getting directions in Paris.

Nala headed further down the hallway wondering how aliens managed to find each other. Clearly, she and Daniel were abysmally equipped for Jheean life. Cave dwellers wandering into the big city without their torches to light the way.

6   OUTSIDE

DANIEL PICKED UP one of the bleached-white bones about the size of a baseball bat and banged it repeatedly against the metal shell of the Jheean megastructure. Each whack produced a dull ring, but the bone finally shattered, stinging his hands as it splintered.

No doors opened.

Sweltering heat surrounded him like an oversized hair dryer. It brought back memories of a June hike to the bottom of the Grand Canyon with temperatures reaching 120 degrees Fahrenheit. Sunbaked rock walls inflicted even more radiation on those who dared to venture that deep. But for canyon hikers, a quick dip in the cold Colorado River provided instant resolution.

No such luck for outdoor enthusiasts from Jheean.

"Maybe you don't know, but humans need water to survive," he said to his mechanical sidekick who leaned back on its grasshopper haunches. The bot was intently focused on its knee joints, carefully picking out individual grains of sand and tossing them aside.

"Water inside," the s-bot finally said. At least it knew what water was.

One survival thought fed to the next. "Wait a second." Daniel unzipped his thermal jacket. Its heating elements had automatically shut off the moment he'd been dumped outside, but a plastic switch sewn to an inside pocket was marked with two icons – a sun and a snowflake. Daniel pushed the switch to the snowflake position and within seconds a chill circulated around his body.

"Ah, that's more like it." The jacket was almost as refreshing as a river plunge – though limited to his torso and arms – but the technology might make the difference between uncomfortable and dead.

Daniel sighed. "Thank you CNSA. Never doubt Chinese design talents."

He knelt next to the s-bot who was still busy picking out grains of sand with clumsy forepaws. "Let me help." Daniel brushed away the sand, his fingers doing a much better job. "Got a little dinged up yourself, huh? How's the heat for you?"

"Sixty-five point one Celsius," the s-bot said.

"Getting hotter, but does it affect you?"

"No."

"But the sand gets in your joints?"

The s-bot's head twitched. "Sand. Not expected. Not protocol."

Daniel inspected each of the creature's joints and brushed until they were clean. "There, you look better now. With some teamwork, we might get out of this mess."

The bot remained silent.

"Look, it's just you and me. We're both in trouble."

"Yes," the bot squeaked.

"So, let's work it out. Can you contact someone? Or find some way to get back in?"

The s-bot looked up to the hinged door they'd both crashed through. Rising on its haunches, the creature looked like it was ready to make a leap but thought better of it and lowered.

"Hey, I've seen you jump, you're pretty good. Give it a shot, you might be able to reach it."

The s-bot raised two metal claws, its large black eyes moving between them. "Not possible."

"You don't think you could pry it open?"

"No." The s-bot's logic was depressing but made sense. Even if it managed to leap as high as the door, there was nothing to hold on to. A quick scratch across its surface wouldn't accomplish much.

"Okay. How about another entrance?"

"None."

"Any windows? There are rocks out here. We could break the glass."

"Domes."

Daniel nodded. "Yeah, I know about the domes, but getting to them would take a grappling hook. Pretty sure neither one of us can climb up smooth metal."

Daniel ran a tongue across dry lips and gazed across the desert. A range of mountains with purple peaks stood out in one direction. White clouds hung near the highest peaks. There weren't any roads or towns. The barren desert was broken only by the shimmer of heat waves.

"Anything out there, or is Jheean all there is?"

"The Wreck," the s-bot said.

"What's that?"

"Colonists."

"Colonists? Are they people?"

"Yes."

"Well, that could be good. Can we get to this place?"

The s-bot raised higher on its haunches and peered over the first of many sand dunes. It raised one metal arm and pointed. "The Wreck."

Daniel craned his neck. There was nothing to see but more sand.

"How far? You know about human measures, right?" The s-bot had already quoted temperature in Celsius.

"Kilometers. Six point four."

Daniel ran a hand across the back of his neck. The searing sun was now almost directly overhead. Days here were likely shorter than on Earth but trying to hold out until sunset probably meant dying in place. With each breath the hot air burned his throat. His thermal jacket was doing a reasonable job of keeping his core temperature from skyrocketing but there was more to desert survival than just avoiding hyperthermia.

"Any water at this wreck?"

"Yes. Water."

Daniel pondered his options. At this point getting back inside seemed hopeless. He could walk the perimeter, but something told him the other side of this petal would look the same. He'd seen Jheean from above, and symmetry seemed to be its defining feature.

A six-kilometer trek across the desert wasn't a great option either. And leaving Jheean would mean leaving Nala, assuming she was still inside somewhere. At least, her body wasn't lying among the pile of bones at the bottom of the disposal chute. He'd take whatever good news he could get.

"Just a sec," Daniel said to his companion.

Among the bones scattered in the sand, a tattered cloth flapped in the hot wind. Daniel pulled at it, withdrawing more cloth buried under sand. He kept pulling until he held a colored stripe about five feet long. It was ripped in places, thin in others, but it might serve as a head covering. Bands of yellow, red, and pink gave it the look of an alien flag that had been flapping far too long in an unforgiving wind.

Daniel wound the soft cloth around his head creating a makeshift turban. It stuck out enough over his forehead to shade his eyes. Tucking in the last bit, the covering held in place.

"How do I look?" The bot's eyes shifted to Daniel and it let out an imperceptible squeak. Daniel took that for approval. Or possibly embarrassment. He patted the s-bot on its head. "How about you? Can you make it to this place?"

"Yes. Mechanic."

"There's a mechanic there?"

"Yes."

"Okay. Handy for you. From my point of view, a tall glass of water would be very welcome right about now." The plunge down the tube had left him dried out, and it was only going to get worse. At least he wouldn't be doing it alone, though it was hard to tell whether his companion was friend, foe, or something in between.

Daniel cocked his head to one side. "Hey, do you have a name?"

"Three one zero zero."

"I'm Daniel, but you already knew that. Three one zero zero. Mind if I call you Tozz?"

The s-bot screeched. Its head vibrated as if shaking off some bad thought. "Not protocol."

Daniel smiled. "Tozz it is."

He set off across the sand in the direction Tozz had pointed hoping the bot was right about an outpost of civilization – and about water. Tozz leaped, covering in one bound the distance Daniel stepped in twenty paces. Their alliance might be uneven and possibly temporary, but at least he had a hiking partner. Possibly a partner strong enough to carry him, should it come to that.

7 GIANT

NALA WANDERED DOWN a corridor as broad as any boulevard back home. On either side, Jheean residents zipped along the wall, riding on glowing boards. As she got closer, the boards looked more like cones of light projected onto the floor.

One stationary circle of light flashed, beckoning her to try the clever but unexplained form of personal transportation. As she studied, a grunt from behind startled her. A round hairy beast raised a fat arm, pointed at the light, and grunted again.

Startled, she took a deep breath and regained composure. "Sorry, I'm new here. Like this?" She stepped onto the oval and touched the wall as she'd seen others doing. A feeling of lifting preceded a smooth acceleration, and she was soon zooming down the hallway at the pace of a brisk jog. Twisting, she waved behind to the rounded being who had now mounted its own light oval. "Thanks for your help!"

She had no idea where she was going, but the ride itself was fantastic. The boulevard stretched ahead without any clear end but having seen Jheean from above she imagined she was progressing down the length of one petal of the flower. At this speed she'd reach its center in minutes.

Nala scrunched her brow. *But how is that going to find Daniel?* The needle-covered mantises had pointed in this direction, but that didn't mean Daniel had gone all the way to the geographic center.

Nala reduced hand pressure, the light oval slowed, and she hopped off. A few seconds later, her hairy friend flew by. There were probably safeguards built into the system to avoid collisions, but like any form of transportation, it required some awareness from both riders and pedestrians. She'd need to be careful. Exactly the opposite of any street at home, the center of this boulevard seemed safer than the edges.

Apparently, the citizens of this multicultural city already knew that. Several helmeted centipedes congregated in a central square formed by the intersection of the boulevard and a smaller cross street.

She'd always been an outgoing person, but everyone had their limits. She'd lifted a few rocks in her life only to be repulsed by the icky bugs that crawled out. "Just be yourself. The last guy was helpful."

The three creatures formed a semicircle. Each stood erect, greenish brown on their backs and pale white on their bellies. Multiple sets of fans hinged from their bodies looking like those little umbrellas they put in tropical drinks. At least a dozen lower fans pushed to the ground, allowing the centipede to maintain balance. Upper, larger fans seemed to exist for expressive gestures that accompanied their animated conversation.

Sounds came from beneath the helmets like the shush of air from a high-pressure hose. The volume and pitch coordinated with fan gestures – circular motions, slaps, and the flapping of the skin between ribs as the umbrella-like appendages opened and closed. Dark visors hid any physical eyes, but the centipedes unquestionably noticed the intruder.

"Uh, hi, I'm Nala." She waved. Their stares remained fixed. "I'm a human. Kind of lost, actually. Can you help?"

The three centipedes tightened their circle, stiffening upper fans. One shushed through its helmet speaker. The others shushed back.

"Sorry, I don't understand. I thought with the helmets maybe you had a translation capability."

There were more of the complex air shushes but none of the creatures made any motion toward her. At least the hairy guy had pointed and grunted. This trio was as aloof as they came, seeming to speak only to each other with no attempt to interact through fan gestures.

A different voice, gentle and soft, sounded from behind. "They won't be of help to you, dear."

Nala spun around. A giant figure loomed above, a lanky creature so tall it reached halfway to the ceiling.

Mostly torso, its narrow core was hidden beneath a finely woven red cloth that wrapped around like a slim dress. A prominent horizontal hump pushed the cloth outward at mid-torso where two thin arms dangled through holes. Below the dress, two spindly legs stood on oval pads.

The lanky giant's clothing swayed as it shifted its weight left and right. Arms and legs visible outside the cloth displayed more bone and ligament than muscle or flesh, with multiple knobby knees and elbows spaced every few feet.

The giant lowered itself by hinging at each of its many joints, eventually shrinking into something like an origami animal made from folds of paper. After a final fold, its impressive stature matched human height.

Its soft head could have easily been borrowed from any cephalopod. Wrinkled, bumpy skin was gray with glints of violet. Two elongated eyes were set widely apart on bulges, their stark green color contrasting with the gray and violet skin. Below the eyes, a mechanical apparatus with tubes and blinking lights protruded where a nose might be.

From a slit below the facial apparatus a gentle voice cooed with the sound of a dove. "I am Theesah-ma."

Nala swallowed hard. Her heart raced. "Hi, I'm Nala."

At one shoulder, a golf-ball sized sphere hovered in midair with a single green light blinking. The folded giant extended a segmented arm toward Nala. "Pleased. So very nice."

The gentle voice provided some measure of relief. Nala took the rounded hand in hers, marveling at the slightly sticky feeling produced by dozens of tiny pink suction cups at its tip. "You speak English."

"Yes. And humans touch hands upon meeting. Yes?"

"We do. Wow, I can't tell you how relieved I am to find someone who speaks my language."

Theesah-ma motioned to the three centipedes, still clustered together, shushing to each other. "Toraks can be insensitive. Please disregard, lovely Nala. Litian-nolos are different."

Theesah-ma moved away from the centipedes, and Nala joined her. "You're Litian-nolo?"

"I am. And you are human. I have studied your form. Learned your language. Humans are new. Such beautiful people." The giant reached out and stroked Nala's hair, a bold move even if they'd been friends for years. "This. So special. The texture. The color. So lovely."

Nala didn't mind the touch. There was nothing to fear and everything to gain from this giant. Nala smoothed her hair back in place. "We came to Jheean to meet with Litian-nolos. Sorry, I'm with my spouse Daniel… well, I'm supposed to be with him, but we got separated. My fault. I'm not sure where he ended up."

Theesah-ma's voice was silky smooth, feminine in pitch. "Daniel Rice?"

"You know him?"

"I have read about him. And you too."

Surprising. Daniel was certainly well known at home, and Nala's role in first contact had been featured in a few magazine articles. But were their names known off world too? She imagined a rack of alien grocery store tabloids. *Secrets of Humanity Exposed!* one headline would declare. Another would showcase indiscreet beach photos of *Earth's Scientific Power Couple*. Nala in her bikini, of course.

"Gee, no pressure. I hope the real thing meets your expectations."

Theesah-ma's tongue-like head curled along its edges. "In person you are delightful. I never imagined."

The compliments, along with her soothing voice, went a long way to overcoming Theesah-ma's curious appearance, a form composed mostly of elbows and knees. Was she a she? She certainly sounded feminine and wore a dress.

Probably terrible indicators of gender. If Litian-nolos even have gender.

Theesah-ma's green eyes closed briefly. "I overheard your questions to the Toraks. You are lost?"

"Sort of. I need to find Daniel. If this were home, we'd just call each other, but our technology doesn't work here."

Theesah-ma reached into a pocket on her red dress and withdrew a blue aluminum wafer. "You have a security token, yes?"

Nala pulled out her own.

Theesah-ma repositioned the sphere that hovered over one shoulder in front of her face. "Does your Daniel also have a token?"

Nala nodded.

The giant cooed to her sphere with different words but the same pleasant voice, and the sphere projected a blue rectangle into the air. White scribbles scrawled across it.

"I see yours. And one other token coded for humans. Assigned to Nikolaus Jensen, currently at the Council of Equivalence."

"That's it? No more?"

"No more." Theesah-ma pointed to the hovering screen. "Only two humans at Jheean."

Nala pondered the new information. Welcome, but puzzling. Was he still up in the glass cocoon? Possible. He might have returned to Beijing. Being Daniel, he'd probably come up with a better strategy than ignoring the direct order of an armed security agent and jumping into a five-mile vertical tube.

She couldn't blame him for being hesitant, but after years of off and on dating and six months of marriage she thought she knew him better. She'd fully expected Daniel to follow and disappointed he hadn't.

"I guess I'm alone then," Nala said.

"You are not," Theesah-ma replied. "You are with me."

Nala pinched her brow. "Wait a second… the token is how you found me. You're the Litian-nolo we were supposed to meet."

Theesah-ma's head curled. "So interesting. The words you use. Your face. So much expression."

The giant stretched knee joints one by one until she towered overhead once again. "No, I am not your contact. Quite the opposite. I tried to prevent your entry. I even sent a security bot to stop you."

****

The sand wasn't deep, but oppressive heat made each step difficult. Daniel's jacket had already maxed out on its cooling capacity. With a brilliant sun just past zenith – afternoon, in colloquial human terms –

the temperature would only be going up. He had stopped asking his mechanical companion for temperature updates an hour ago.

Daniel took the last few steps to a sandy rise and stopped to survey the surroundings. In the distance, a settlement broke the monotony of barren desert landscape. Trees, faintly purple in color, intermixed with several metal structures, one that stuck above the rest. Beyond the settlement, the desert ended abruptly at a turquoise bay bounded by rocky outcrops.

"Is that it?" Daniel asked, rubbing parched lips.

His companion leaped up to the rise and stretched high on his hind legs. "Yes. The Wreck."

Daniel stared at the metal grasshopper who rarely put more than two words together but seemed to understand everything Daniel said. "You know, Tozz, you're pretty good at communication."

Three one zero zero twitched its head in a move somewhere between irritation and I've-got-water-in-my-ear but made no attempt to correct the name Daniel had assigned. "Human language. Downloaded."

"Well, keep up the good work." Daniel stared out across the dry landscape, shimmering heatwaves making the distant buildings look like one of those mining towns on a lonely highway in Nevada. A town like Tonopah, for example. Daniel knew it well.

He thought of home. Not Tonopah specifically, but Earth in general. It kept his mind off the heat and a throat so dry it hurt. Symptoms of heat stroke hadn't yet appeared thanks to the thermal jacket, but its crippling effects could strike at any time. Once dizziness and nausea set in, any hiker in these temperatures wouldn't get much farther.

Twenty long minutes later the trees were close enough to make out their shapes. Palms of some kind – a bare stalk with foliage at the top.

Their deep purple contrasted with turquoise water and a rust red shoreline that fronted the settlement. It felt like a badly colorized version of Baja California or Saudi Arabia. It also felt uncomfortably familiar.

He shoved the thought aside. Negativity was a powerful killer when the mind needed to stay sharp. His dream wasn't materializing. Fate wasn't real. He'd learned that lesson from a preacher called Father in a timeline that no longer existed.

One structure stood above the rest, looking like a sharp mountain peak with striated layers. The skewed layers pitched diagonally to flat land, like a building that had been pushed over by a rampaging Godzilla.

With inviting waters ahead, the worst of the hike was over but that didn't stop each hot breath from searing his lungs. Air conditioning might be too much to ask for, but the shade of the trees would be welcome.

A few minutes later, Daniel finally stepped onto a pink concrete platform. Overhead, someone had stretched the ragged remains of a parachute between two palms. A rock wall surrounded the encampment, but one crumbled section served as a neglected gate. Daniel stepped through the scattered rocks. It was no Jheean, but the water was no mirage.

A stone pathway led past a small building constructed of scrap metal. Sheets of irregular shapes and sizes were welded together in a haphazard patchwork. On the other side of the ramshackle building, the path opened to a sandy beach fronting turquoise water where small waves lapped against the shore. Palms ran in a straight line in one direction. Beyond them, wreckage of an enormous ship rose from the sand.

Twice the height of the tallest tree, the wreck's pointy top could have easily been the bow of any ocean-going vessel on Earth, but its wings – lopsided, with a wingtip sheared off on one side – spoke to a different mode of transportation. Another chunk of twisted metal was partially buried in sand away from the main fuselage, with several smaller pieces scattered further down the beach. Waves broke against the wreckage without moving it in the slightest.

For now, Daniel ignored the fascinating scene of some long-ago disaster. His focus was more on the water, but his heart sank as white froth stirred up when a wave broke. He sprinted the last few steps, splashing into the water. Shallow and warm, it was the foam that worried him most.

"It's water?" he asked as Tozz caught up.

"Water," Tozz replied.

"Dihydrogen monoxide? H_2O. That kind of water?"

"Yes."

"Any other chemicals?"

"Sodium."

Daniel shook his head. "I was afraid you were going to say that." Disappointed, he lifted a palmful of water to his lips and tasted. Salty. "Sorry Tozz, that's not going to work. My mistake not yours. I asked for water, and you led me to it."

Daniel did his best to calm the rising feeling of panic. It was undrinkable, but even warm saltwater could provide evaporative cooling. Daniel soaked himself up to his hips, took off his makeshift turban and soaked it too. Drips ran down his neck as he secured the wet rag back over his head.

"Feels good." Daniel sloshed back to the sand and sat down in the shade of one of the palms feeling instant relief from the heat even if his throat was still parched. He stared down the beach at the colossal wreckage of some unfortunate space pilot. "I see why you call it the Wreck."

He pointed a thumb to the ramshackle building higher on the sandy beach. Its front side was no different, a patchwork of sheet metal scraps and a few palm tree trunks. More parachute material had been strung between palms. If there were any windows or doors, they'd been boarded up.

"Any chance we'll find water inside? Without sodium?" There was no one around and the building looked like it hadn't been occupied in years. If there was water stored inside, a break-in would be justified. He'd tear the sheet metal off with bare hands if he had to.

Tozz hopped to the building and inspected beneath an eave. Rusted metal bars ran horizontally – a potential doorway, though blocked. The s-bot's glassy eyes turned back to Daniel. "Stay here." The bot leaped down the beach, past the wreckage, and within a minute had disappeared around a rocky prominence.

Daniel was perfectly willing to stay put. Too tired to follow and too hot to leave the shade of the palm. His thirst was intense, but he was willing to give Tozz a few minutes before trying to break into the building.

Daniel leaned against the base of the palm. His pants and head gear were still wet though drying rapidly. Evaporative cooling and his thermal jacket would prevent heat stroke, but dehydration still loomed large.

He stared up to the blue sky, transfixed by flashes of sunlight that filtered through the cracks in the palm fronds as they rustled in the breeze. A hint of orange in the sunlight contrasted with the darker purple of the frond.

Red dwarf star, common. But retinal-based plants, uncommon.

Science came to him at the oddest moments, apparently even when struggling for his life. On Earth, retinal produced the distinctive purple color that some plants have, a color that most paleobotanists believe dominated plants a billion years ago. But life evolved, and retinal lost out to the more efficient chlorophyll molecule.

Maybe retinal still dominated here. The distant mountains were purple at their peaks. Daniel lifted a handful of sand and let it pour slowly through his fingers. It was time to face facts.

I'm living the dream.

An odd way to put it, but this moment was playing out precisely as he'd dreamt it over several months. Alone on a hot beach. A purple palm and a turquoise sea. Intense thirst and a handful of sand. Had the repeating dream been a vision of this moment? A premonition of his pending death?

Or time entanglement?

It was only Zin's guess. But a scientific rationale no matter how tenuous was more satisfying than a Greek oracle's prophesy. An explanation also provided hope that death wasn't imminent. There had been other visions too – a hooded figure, a soothing voice, a beveled disc of glass – but nothing like these images had yet occurred. Maybe they represented real events in his future.

Assuming I have a future.

Daniel gazed up. Repetitive flashes of sunlight through palm fronds were mesmerizing. Calming. For a moment, at least, he forgot about his thirst and the heat.

Eyelids heavy, the rest of his body suddenly felt light. Weightless, as if he had lifted a few inches off the sand. Perhaps it was delirium brought on by dehydration. Daniel was conscious, not asleep. Aware, but spellbound on the flickering light overhead.

The sky darkened. Daniel floated in space. His feet touched nothing. A band of stars, dust, and nebulae splashed across the sky forming a dreamy display of galactic glory. To one side, an enormous disc of glass floated in space, its beveled edges sparkling like a diamond. From the disc's center, a narrow beam of red light blazed out across the starry sky.

He heard a voice. Female, and silky smooth. "It draws the eye."

Daniel turned toward the curious voice. A shape loomed, tall and thin. Real but indistinct. More outline than solid but very much alive.

It was another repetition of a vision he'd had before. This time he could make out the words. "Who are you?" he asked for the first time.

The outline floated nearby but ignored Daniel as if he didn't exist, speaking with a wistful longing for an answer to some long-sought question. "We left to stay behind, they say. Still a puzzle."

The daydream faded. The splash of stars washed away replaced by a palm tree that arced overhead. Sunlight peaked between palm fronds. Sharp pain from a parched throat returned. Heat waves shimmered over the turquoise sea. But the words still echoed in his mind.

We left to stay behind.

Nonsensical. Certainly confusing. The illogical words lodged in Daniel's mind like a tickle that would eventually need to be scratched. He wasn't going to die. Not today. There was a puzzle to be solved.

8   COLONIST

"*YOU* SENT THE s-bot to stop us from entering Jheean?"

Nala barely reached to the hemline of Theesah-ma's red dress. At full height, the Litian-nolo was intimidating even though her voice remained silky soft.

"I did. Jheean is not safe for you. Or your Daniel."

Nobody had mentioned anything about danger inside the alien megacity. Not Zin, not Secretary Jensen. Not even the s-bot, whose high-pitched squeals had been more irritating than threatening. If there were dangers, they were well hidden within the sometimes confusing but benign community.

But if anyone at Jheean could be trusted to speak truth it was probably Theesah-ma. She'd been kind from the moment they'd met. Of course, Nala's trust could easily be a byproduct of the alien's naturally soothing voice.

Zin would have good advice about who to trust and who to avoid, but somehow the android was always missing just when he was most needed. Handing out walkie-talkies might have been more useful than security wafers.

The lanky giant refolded surprisingly agile joints until it had once more compressed to its smallest form. "The gravity here is difficult for me. Adjustments help."

"Feels light for me, but you're so slender it must be hard just to keep upright." Nala motioned to the apparatus on her face. "For breathing or speaking?"

"Breathing. An addition of hydrogen sulfide. Necessary for us. The gas is not present in this sector." Her torso hump shifted like she was stretching sore shoulders. Her green eyes rolled independently from each other but locked in coordination when she looked at Nala. "I come to Jheean when required. Important this time."

"To prevent Daniel and me from entering... which I might point out didn't work."

"Yes, you are here. But Daniel is not. He must not enter."

"Why?"

"Humans are new. With much to learn. Lovely Nala, I too am a scientist. I report to Seishu-kai-do, a diplomat for Litian-nolos and your contact. Seishu-kai-do expected to greet you. But I intervened. My reasons are complex. Please know that Litian-nolos are not of one mind."

"Neither are humans."

"I understand. As does Seishu-kai-do. At this moment, he advocates for humans at the Council of Equivalence. Others oppose. If the Council rejects you, it will be a terrible mistake. Avoidance does not teach. Even for people who are dangerous."

There had been rumors that the history of warfare on Earth had become a sticking point in humanity's quest for membership.

"Do you think we're dangerous?"

Theesah-ma remained silent for a moment. "Yes. Possibly. The wars. The weapons. These are not good for any people. But barriers are not the answer. There is no learning in distance. The Sandzvallons were shunned. They did not learn. And now they are scavengers."

Nala remembered an entire evening discussing the tragedy with Daniel. According to Zin, the Sandzvallons of Gamma Carinae were a promising species that had toyed with the power of time travel and lost everything, their civilization now in ruins.

"Humans must learn too. Weapons must remain within boundaries." Theesah-ma gently brushed Nala's cheek. "You are more beautiful than your photographs. Please, do not destroy yourselves."

"I hope we don't. Maybe you can help us."

"Seishu-kai-do has suggested just such an answer. Like you, Litian-nolos are curious people. We have studied you. We see your promise and your danger. I tell you this to make you aware. But it is not why I intervened."

"To keep us safe. From the Toraks?"

"From forces you cannot understand."

"Try me. I'm smart."

Theesah-ma curled the edges of her head. "You *are* smart. Now that I have met you, this fact is clearer. Yet, I worry for you. Do you know the art of time manipulation, lovely Nala?"

"Not me personally, no. Or Daniel for that matter. But we've heard that Litian-nolos manipulate timelines. It's why we're here. Our guide, Zin, thought Daniel might be time entangled, whatever that is."

"Worse, I am afraid. An inflection point comes soon. One of our time mentors, Hataki-ka, has foreseen it. Hataki-ka warned me. Your Daniel may be the instigator and must be stopped."

In mathematics, an inflection point marked the position on a curving line as it bends one way and then another. Business leaders talked about inflection points as subtle changes in a marketplace or customer demand. The concept could certainly be applied to the delicate shifts that might ripple through a timeline, but Theesah-ma might have her own meaning.

"Is an inflection point bad?"

"Good or bad. But altering on a large scale. Clarity will come only when the event arrives."

"And Daniel caused this large scale whatever?"

"Cause and effect do not apply. An instigator is entangled. An instigator manipulates a timeline. Sometimes by accident."

"If Daniel had anything to do with altering timelines, I can assure you it was by accident."

"You cannot know this. The events have not yet occurred."

Time craziness was rearing its ugly head again. "But they will? At this upcoming inflection point?"

"Yes… or no. Not even time mentors can be sure."

A rapidly flashing light on the sphere that hovered near Theesah-ma's shoulder interrupted. She gave a voice command and a blue rectangle appeared in the air. Alien writing was scrawled across its surface.

"Oh, dear."

"What?"

"A notification from the Jheean security system. A third human token was issued but is missing."

Nala nodded. "Which makes sense. Daniel had a token but returned to Earth. He probably took it with him."

Theesah-ma was quick to contradict. "He did not. Tokens continuously report their position." Theesah-ma squinted. "At last report, this token was ejected from a disposal chute."

"Ejected? Like to a garbage dumpster?"

"Ejected outside the Jheean citadel. Rare. Most materials are recycled. But not all."

Nerves tingled. Nala's fighting instincts flared. "You're suggesting Daniel may have been thrown outside?"

"Yes. Outside is a grave danger. A thermal dead zone. Litian-nolos would die within minutes. Humans have greater resistance, but we must find him."

Nala put a hand over her mouth. She would give anything for the report to be mistaken but something about Theesah-ma's nervous stance rang true. Theesah-ma had predicted danger. She'd even sent an s-bot to prevent their entry. And now, things had gone terribly wrong for Daniel.

My fault. I forced him to jump.

She was a novice in a foreign place. Even with a sympathetic ear, Nala knew she'd need as much help as she could get. "Show me how that sphere of yours works. I need to reach Zin."

****

Daniel felt a shove and opened his eyes. Blurred vision made it difficult to make out the face, but a beak like a hawk's stood out from under a white canvas hood. The hawk creature pushed again.

"Yeah… I, uh can't…" A thick tongue prevented much more.

A dribble of cool water ran in and out of his open mouth. He swallowed, anxious for more. No hallucination, the water continued to flow. He drank as fast as it poured. Grabbing at a leathery bag, Daniel tipped its neck and let the water pour in between breaths. He got to his knees, wiped his chin, and allowed crusty eyes to refocus.

He was still on sand in the shade of a palm. Next to Tozz was a hunched figure dressed in white robes. Humanoid in shape, except for the prominent beak that stood out from a hooded face.

"Thank you," Daniel gasped. He drank another slug of water, then handed the bag back. The figure seized it with a bird-like claw.

Tozz hopped next to Daniel and pressed forepaws under his armpits. The s-bot rose on its haunches, lifting Daniel to a standing position.

Somewhat shorter than Daniel, the white robed figure was bent at its waist with a curving back. A metal ball hovered in midair at its shoulder, its position fixed even as the robed figure moved. Beneath the folds of its hood, a weathered face peaked out. Heavily wrinkled skin and slit-like eyes sat above the prominent beak that protruded several inches, as fierce as any bird of prey but flexible enough to form words.

"Drangen koolt," the wrinkled bird said.

Tozz poked a forepaw at Daniel's leg and squeaked, "Drangen sheeb. Dix nbor."

Daniel did his best to repeat the foreign words, which brought a squint to the birdman's eyes and a grunt from its beak. A claw grabbed the hovering sphere and repositioned it between them. A single light blinked on its surface.

His voice was deep and rough with age. "Peej doog asa kanda." He lifted a bird claw to his beak, then pointed to Daniel.

"You want me to talk?" Daniel replied. The sphere blinked several times as if it had accepted Daniel's sample, then produced sounds very much like those that the birdman had spoken.

The birdman scratched out more words, and an English translation sounded from the hovering device. "I want you to live. No one dies at the Wreck. Not if I can help it."

Daniel bowed his head, grateful for communication and so much more. He locked eyes with the narrow slits peering from under the hood.

The hooded figure from my dreams?

He'd seen these robes before but without the intricate detail of woven patterns now made vivid by reality. Daniel swallowed, thankful the pain in his throat had diminished. "You saved my life. I'm in your debt."

Translations came quickly. "The s-bot saved your life. I brought only water."

Daniel patted Tozz on its metal head, his fingers recoiling from the hot surface. "Is there a cooler place we can go?"

The birdman nodded once, then turned toward the ramshackle building at the top of the sandy beach. As he walked, the spherical device dutifully returned to his shoulder. Daniel and Tozz followed.

A six-legged hooved animal fitted with a saddle stood tied to a post. It hadn't been there before. It might even represent transportation back to Jheean if they could find a ground-level entrance to the megastructure. The birdman might know.

The robed man pulled a keyring from the saddle and ambled down several steps under an eave. Rusted bars blocked an entryway. Once unlocked, the gate rolled into a wooden frame, and the birdman shoved open a flimsy door.

The building was dark inside with a jumbled architecture. Bent I-beams served as posts to hold the roof up. The floor stepped down then back up at random intervals. Doorways led to other rooms like afterthoughts in its construction.

A fan engaged, blowing cool air. Not enough to eliminate the oppressive heat but Daniel's thermal jacket would take care of the rest. He removed the damp rag from his head.

They entered a larger room with a low ceiling of roughhewn wood beams. A narrow tabletop split the room with stools of varying heights on either side. The birdman dropped the water bag on the table and motioned to Daniel to take a stool. Tozz squatted next to Daniel, its hot metal skin creaking as it cooled.

"You okay?" Daniel asked the s-bot.

"Polymer," it answered. "Mechanic."

Daniel pointed to the birdman who was rummaging through an open cupboard stacked with bottles. "He's the mechanic?"

"Yes," Tozz answered. The s-bot flicked a few more grains of sand off one leg, but tiny beads of an oily substance now appeared at its joints. Silicone was a polymer. Maybe Tozz had gotten a WD-40 rubdown.

Daniel took another swig of water from the bag. "It seems we both owe you. My name is Daniel."

The birdman turned around, setting a bottle of red liquid on the table along with two small glasses. "I am Ajadu. I have heard rumors of humans even before your s-bot fetched me, but you are the first I have seen."

"As far as I know, we're the first humans to visit your planet."

"Not my planet."

Daniel stared quizzically. "But this is your place?" It didn't look like a home, more like a bar, especially with all the bottles. Daniel had a hard time imagining where customers would come from.

"The proprietor." He poured red liquid from the bottle into a glass. "Jurg. The nectar of life. Will you join me?"

"Happy to, as long as it doesn't kill me."

The old birdman took a large sip from the glass. His slit eyes closed for a moment as the liquid performed its magic. "Made from a plant that grows in the mountains. Aged for three seasons. If jurg kills you, you will die happy."

Daniel lifted the glass to his lips, and a strong fragrance of honey filled his nostrils. If it tasted as good, Ajadu might be right about the nectar of life. Daniel took the smallest of sips, feeling his tongue go numb then a prickle in his cheeks. "Tingly. But strangely refreshing."

"You will never drink water again," Ajadu said. "Without jurg, I would have left this barren inferno long ago."

Daniel took a larger sip. A frosty sensation followed the liquid down his esophagus. "Like drinking liquid nitrogen." His voice came out at an unusually high pitch.

A shared drink with the person who'd saved his life was the least Daniel could do, regardless of risk. Poisoning was unlikely. Drunkenness was a distinct possibility, but he'd worry about that later. "If this isn't your planet then where's home?"

"I am a Colonist. We live most everywhere. My birthplace is not far, but it takes a fast starship to get there."

"Like the wreck out front?"

"My grandfather's. A miner who came to Bektash in search of a rare metal. He found it. Too much. The ship was overweight and crashed on takeoff. His competitors looted every bit of..." He thumped Tozz on the head. "What do humans call A46?"

"Palladium," Tozz answered.

"The forty-sixth element," Daniel answered. "A rare metal on Earth."

"Plentiful on Bektash. At least it used to be. Much of the A46 went to build that hexagon monstrosity. To reinforce their glass."

"Ah, so that's why Jheean is here."

The birdman sneered. "A den of thieves and liars. I prefer the desert." He took another sip of jurg, then a second for good measure. "I salvaged my grandfather's wreck to build this place along with a cliff house further along the shore. Forty seasons I have been here." He rapped a startled Tozz. "How long is that in their measures?"

"Six hundred seventy-four years," Tozz answered.

Daniel thought he'd heard the number wrong, but then looked again at the deep creases on the birdman's face. *Was such age possible?*

"These days we hold an occasional Colonist gathering here, though most of the miners have scattered to other outposts. Some sell their wares at... *Jheean*." He spit the name out like a spoiled batch of jurg. "Like others, Colonists have a diplomat or two there, for whatever good it does us." If Ajadu's broken-down building was any indication, Colonists lived impoverished lives compared to the technology-laden luxury inside Jheean.

"Interesting." Daniel had thought this planet served only as a gathering place for the twenty-three species of Sagittarius Novus, but it was clear Bektash had its own history, possibly a long one. "Why the Colonist name?"

"It's probably just the sphere's translation. In your language it might come out as colonist, wanderer, settler. Close enough. But literally..." Ajadu squeezed the hovering sphere, then spoke in his native language. "Asa klage ni tjab." Releasing pressure, the sphere translated word for word, "we left to stay behind."

Hairs prickled across Daniel's neck as the words from his heatstroke delusion sounded once more.

We left to stay behind, they say. Still a puzzle. Daniel's memory rarely failed. The curious expression matched the vision, just as Ajadu's hooded robe had.

Cause before effect. Daniel had witnessed the illogical sequence of events in his time travels. The sequence now unfolding at the Wreck was starting to feel eerily similar, confirming the images had been more than just dreams.

Daniel chose his words carefully. "This is going to sound strange, but I've heard that phrase before. In a daydream. Repeated just minutes ago, before you found me."

"You dreamt the Colonist name?"

"Yes, those exact words. We left to stay behind. I thought it was the heat, but now… The phrase doesn't make sense, which is why it stuck in my mind. Who leaves to stay behind?"

Ajadu stood up and circled Daniel, examining him from all sides. "Are humans visionaries?"

"Visionaries in some ways, but no, we don't normally see or hear things that pop up a few minutes later." *Unless you're an entangled time traveler*, but Daniel held his tongue on that reveal. He was still processing it himself. Ajadu was likely the hooded figure of his dreams, though the protruding beak was new. Some dream details seemed to be filling in as events unfolded.

Ajadu pushed his empty glass aside and leaned on the table, peering into Daniel's face. "In this vision, what else did you see?"

If Ajadu was a part of this sequence of events, it made sense to play the scene to its conclusion. Time to tell all.

"Well, I'm floating in space. Stars – the Milky Way, I guess – are spread out across the sky. Nearby is a large disc of glass with beveled jewel edges and a red laser projecting from it. There's someone else there, too – mostly a voice. Not human, but probably not a Colonist either. It seemed to be calling attention to the laser. 'It draws the eye', the voice said."

Ajadu plunked onto his stool. "Very true. It does draw the eye."

Daniel paused, blinking. Cause before effect might not be the only issue. Either Ajadu knew something or the jurg was kicking in. "How...?"

"I am no seer, but your words are not difficult to recognize. Perhaps there is more going on than you understand." Ajadu poured another round of the red liquid into both glasses. "Drink up, my human friend. You must return to the Jheean citadel, and I will take you there myself. But before we leave, I have a story to tell. By the end I predict you will understand this vision of yours. And perhaps much more."

9   ANCIENTS

DANIEL SAT AT the edge of his bar stool. If Ajadu had a plan to get back inside Jheean – what he'd called the citadel – Daniel was onboard. The sooner the better. The more he learned about this place, the more he worried that Nala had met with trouble too.

But a tantalizing clue suggested Ajadu might also have an answer to Daniel's mental predicament. According to Ajadu, *we left to stay behind*, was the literal translation of the Colonists' name. Those precise words had sounded in the delirium version of Daniel's starfield vision.

Ajadu had also said there was more going on than Daniel understood. Almost certainly true. Daniel settled in while Ajadu spoke.

"My story is ancient, and so are the players." Ajadu's translated voice came from the hovering sphere at his shoulder. So far, the device had performed flawlessly.

The old birdman pulled his hood back. Wrinkles across his weathered skin continued around both sides of his head, and speckles of white age spots appeared along both sides of his neck. Even his hawk-like beak had chips in it.

"Forty seasons on Bektash, and I was eleven when my grandfather brought me here. Fifty-one seasons, a long life by almost any measure."

Ajadu raised a claw, but before he could rap the s-bot's head Tozz dutifully translated. "Eight hundred sixty years."

The old man's age was impressive if the number could be believed. On Earth, some pines and cypress trees could survive for several thousand years. Coral too, which is technically an animal. But any species with a high metabolic rate – mammals, birds, or reptiles –

maxed out around two hundred years. Death was inevitable when DNA replication degraded with each cell division. Perhaps the Colonists' genetic molecule was sturdier.

But there was another alternative, and Daniel asked, "Do your people engineer their genetic code?"

"Long ago, yes." Ajadu dipped his head. "My ancestors became quite successful at it, and their lifespan increased dramatically. Every few generations they reinforced the changes. Others may scoff, but in those early days, Colonists lived as long as six thousand seasons."

Daniel glanced at Tozz, who computed the answer quickly. "One hundred thousand years."

Daniel raised a brow, unsure how much of this story might be fable. There was no reason to challenge the old birdman. He'd provided water and shelter. A good yarn came with the territory.

"Does anyone really want to live that long? I can't imagine I would."

"Want or need?" Ajadu queried. "These were days before the compression of space. Traveling great distances required a fast starship, but even with the best of technologies a trip to a habitable planetary system could take a hundred seasons. A thousand for a longer voyage. My ancestors, who some call the Ancients, altered their lifespans to meet the conditions they faced."

"Ah," Daniel said, taking another sip of the ridiculously cold jurg. His body had mostly recovered from the heat, but the occasional reinforcement of frozen honey couldn't hurt. "Your ancestors were in the same position as humans. With telescopes, we discovered thousands of planets, but travel was beyond our abilities – and our lifetimes. But if you lived for a hundred thousand years…"

"Space travel is never easy. My ancestors struggled. Today, we have only scraps – stories passed down from one generation to the next. Stories of a home planet called Dissat. Of valiant starship captains plying the emptiness of space. Of the first Colonists who established outposts and set up trade routes. Great achievements made possible by the gift of long life. People are willing to endure the hardships of space travel when they will live to see the destination."

"No stasis, then. No cryogenics." Daniel hoped the technical terms would translate to something Ajadu might recognize.

"Suspension of life? No. Our ancestors never accomplished such a miracle. We became wanderers, but our genetic advantage became the reason those ancient voyages ended."

"Your ancestors stopped exploring?"

"Perhaps. Only they would know. You see, there is a second part to this story. The Great Divide. A troubled time in our history. Some wanted to wander. To seek out life in distant places. Others wanted to settle. Our people split into two factions. One group began a long voyage, the greatest of all journeys. The rest stayed behind."

Daniel spoke the vision words once more. "We left to stay behind."

"Yes, our name comes from the Great Divide. But there is more. Colonists ended the madness of genetic alteration, a major point of contention among our people. Our ancestors had raised self-manipulation to a religion. The Designer, they called their god, the greatest genetic engineer of all time. They mimicked their god's handiwork, not only in their own bodies but with other species too – even crafting new species that never existed.

"Since the divide, Colonists have banished genetic manipulation, but the legends from our history are not as easily erased. Over time, our lifespans have reverted, each generation becoming closer to our natural state. I may live to eighty seasons – still a long time compared to any species – but far shorter than six thousand. Colonists of today now find comfort that our lifetimes will end. A person can only experience so much of the world before it becomes repetitive."

"I completely understand," Daniel acknowledged. Even eight hundred years seemed enough for anyone. A hundred thousand would get tedious.

"But there is more you must understand. During the turmoil of this period, my ancestors agreed to make a final alteration to their genes. Storytelling is in our culture. This final change would explain the divide to future generations." Ajadu pulled his robes down across shoulders and turned to show Daniel his back.

His dark skin was randomly speckled with lighter spots on either side, but in the center a bright white line about two inches wide vertically bisected his back. Halfway down, the line split in two, with both lines continuing in parallel like prongs on a tuning fork. It didn't look like a tattoo and there was little chance that natural mutation could cause such a striking design of skin pigmentation.

"Your ancestors put a diagram of the Great Divide into your genes?" Daniel asked, incredulous that such a story-telling method could exist.

Ajadu pulled the white robe back into place and faced Daniel. "It is the Colonists' mark. We all have it from birth, a reminder of who we once were."

Daniel grabbed the bottle of jurg and poured another round, taking a large slug of the frosty drink. The visual confirmation of Ajadu's story was astonishing, but the birdman wasn't just being conversational.

He knows something.

"Ajadu, your story is an honor to your history and your people. I feel your pride and your sense of connection to the past. But I think you're showing me the mark for a reason. It's related to my dream?"

Ajadu stood up and paced, his spherical ball following within a few feet of his body. "Humans are new, but I sense something unique in you. As if our story is yours too."

Daniel shook his head. "Humans have no knowledge of your ancient past, or any other civilization. Until just a few years ago, we thought we were alone in this universe."

"But your vision tells you otherwise."

"My vision could have been the heat."

"I think not. Your vision taught you the words of the Ancients and showed you our most sacred place, the beacon."

"The beacon?"

Ajadu nodded slowly. "In your vision, you floated in space. You saw a circle of glass with jeweled facets around its edge. You saw a red light that reached across the stars. *It draws the eye*, a voice told you. You have been there, Daniel, if only in your mind. It is a place unique in this galaxy. Sacred to all Colonists because it was constructed by our ancestors, the Ancients of the planet Dissat. Their work started long ago and finished before the Great Divide. Today, we call this place the Star Beacon."

"It still exists?"

"It is a landmark known by every species of Sagittarius Novus and revered by all for its ancient origins. Other species pretend that little is understood about its construction, but we Colonists know better. The Star Beacon is ours. It always was."

"A beacon of red light. For what purpose?"

"Communication. A search for others. There are many theories, but you must understand my ancestors were like you. At the time, they believed they were alone in the universe. The Ancients were the first people, the original technical civilization of this galaxy. They came before any of the species that now form Sagittarius Novus." Ajadu motioned to Tozz. "Tell him."

Tozz snapped to attention like he'd been dozing off. "Star Beacon. Zone 3B, quadrant 17. Orbiting star Z4942. Estimated age, 25 million Earth years."

Even though Daniel had just absorbed a story about long lifetimes and ancient events, the number was stunning. "Technology that is twenty-five *million* years old. You're sure?"

"Yes," Tozz replied. "Age verified. Star Beacon abandoned 4.8 million years ago. When the Ancients disappeared."

Ajadu added. "Your s-bot echoes the common belief of Sagittarius Novus members, that the Ancients *disappeared*. Technically true, but it does not tell the story that I have just told you. The Ancients *are* the Colonists. One and the same, though our people diverged nearly five million years ago. The Colonists of today settled across a collection of planets, including Bektash. The others left. Where they went, we do not know."

Ajadu studied Daniel as if searching for something in his expression. "We Colonists are adept at interpreting stories that span generations, even stories still in progress. You envisioned the Star Beacon, of that, I am sure. But why? I sense something else. Something deeper. My friend, I may not know where the Ancients went, but I believe you do."

****

Nala sped down Jheean's central avenue riding an oval of light with Theesah-ma in front. The giant Litian-nolo remained in her folded origami position. They ventured deeper into the colossal structure, past market areas teeming with alien people of all shapes, past intricately carved stone monoliths that served some unknown function – or might simply be art. Dozens of alleyways splintering from the main avenue gave a sense of being a small mouse in a large maze.

You're such an idiot.

She'd jumped into the Jheean entry tube without giving Daniel any chance to argue the merits of sneaking in by way of the backdoor. She knew he'd follow, and he had – only to be thrown unceremoniously into the desert along with whatever other junk was unworthy of Jheean tenancy. Security procedures that could allow such abuse made her blood boil, but she reserved most of her anger for herself. She'd gotten Daniel into this mess.

Somehow, he would survive. Daniel was good at things like that, but he was probably suffering. She'd do anything to reset, but now her best option was to get Zin involved. Theesah-ma had been a lifesaver in that department, easily locating Zin and sending a message via her floating sphere.

Meet me outside the central hex, Zin had responded. Nala had no idea how to get to the rendezvous point but Theesah-ma did.

Without any command from its rider, each light oval made a jog to the left. The path straightened once more, and a dark wall loomed ahead. Theesah-ma slowed and hopped off. Nala did the same.

They stood at the base of an imposing black barrier that stretched indefinitely to the left and right. The giant unfolded, stretching limbs and joints that seemed to be always sore. At her full size, Theesah-ma was still only half the fortification's height. King Kong would have struggled to get past this barrier.

"The central hexagon," Theesah-ma announced. "One of six sides."

The dark surface was uneven, as if it had been built from bricks of varying sizes. Several rounded hemispheres – also black – stuck out from the wall, adding to its randomness. Theesah-ma stepped toward a particularly large hemisphere at floor level. Three s-bots stood at attention.

"The entryway. We have no authorization to continue, but your Zin will meet us here."

Every second was agony, but finally the hemisphere split down the middle and a shiny android stepped through its opening. Zin hurried over to Nala.

"So sorry to hear!" Zin was as animated as she'd ever seen him. The unibrow over his flat metal eyes twisted into an unnatural display of concern.

There was no time for platitudes. Nala answered, "How do we get him back inside?"

Zin fretted. "I wish I knew. We'll need to find Dr. Rice first, a task made difficult by Jheean design. These walls deliberately isolate us from a fierce desert with few inhabitants and low technology. Many have perished outside. I so regret my involvement in this terrible situation."

Nala put a hand on his metal arm. She needed his experience, not his anxiety about handing out security passes. "Daniel's smart. He'll find a way, but we need to give him a chance. Are there access points where he could get back in? A door we can unlock?"

"Possibly," Zin answered. "I contacted Core on my way here about this unfortunate transgression. Apparently, Core spoke with Daniel through an s-bot assigned by the Council, but what happened after that is still a mystery. Council decisions are not subject to overruling and even if they were Core wouldn't –".

Nala cut him off. "Fuck Core. Fuck the Council. Fuck every fucked-up security protocol this place has established." Zin could spend half the day explaining things but at this moment, they needed action. Her harsh words had the intended effect, and Zin shut up.

Nala was softer this time, but firm. "Now, how do we help Daniel?"

The android's eyes flickered. "The Bektash desert is extensive, but my organic molecular scanning subsystem could distinguish human flesh from the local flora. And has a range of at least three kilometers." He glanced at Theesah-ma, then Nala. "I suggest we start at the disposal chute."

"Then lead the way."

Fortunately, the route was short. Light ovals brought them to the disposal chute in less than a minute. Zin performed some magic at a wall-mounted controller, and a large glass panel swung open. Hot air drifted in, feeling no different than if they'd opened an oven door.

Nala, Theesah-ma, and Zin all leaned in. The chute plunged several meters to a brightly lit opening. Beyond was the dusty surface of the planet Bektash.

"Ugh," Zin said, climbing into the chute. "Sand."

10 BACKDOOR

AJADU'S EXPLANATION of the Ancients, the Great Divide, and the Colonists' mark no doubt harbored some truth within the fable, but the story had ended with nonsense.

Daniel countered the old birdman's claim. "I have no idea where the Ancients went. How could I?"

His head down, Ajadu rummaged through several crates in the corner of his ramshackle bar. "Visionaries often fail to recognize their talent."

"Sorry to disappoint you, but I'm not a visionary either. My dreams are just..." He had to admit he didn't know what they were. Two had already become reality – dying of thirst on a seashore, and a mysterious hooded figure who had turned out to be Daniel's rescuer. There was a distinct possibility the remaining dream fragments might resolve to reality too. The starry sky, the beveled disc of glass, and a red laser that Ajadu claimed was a real place called the Star Beacon.

"Like it or not, you are a visionary. And it is my duty to return you to the Jheean citadel."

Daniel couldn't get there soon enough. He'd allow the old birdman his eccentricities if it provided a path across the dangerous desert. Tozz had just returned from a peek outside and reported 71 Celsius, 160 Fahrenheit. Even riding on Ajadu's hooved beast, that kind of heat would be hard to survive.

"Perhaps we should wait until nightfall?"

Ajadu dug deeper into one crate, tossing around contents that clanked and thumped. "You would not care to meet the night dwellers of Bektash. The razorfins along our route will be bad enough." He returned with two coils of metal wire that reminded Daniel of slinky toys. "Do humans breathe under water?"

Daniel instinctively ran fingers across his neck to demonstrate the lack of gills. "Not really. We can hold air in our lungs for a brief submersion, but we need to surface regularly."

Ajadu's proposed pathway back to Jheean sounded wet. The turquoise sea was only a few steps across a hot beach, but if their route involved swimming upstream through an alien sewage pipe Daniel might seek other options.

Ajadu dropped the slinky coils on the table. Each circle of wire threaded through to a black bar that ran the length of the coil. A white strap completed the setup. He demonstrated its use by placing the coil behind his head and wrapping the white strap around his thin neck, essentially creating a slinky backpack. Daniel did the same, tightening a buckle at the strap's front but keeping enough slack to avoid cutting off circulation.

Ajadu returned to the crates and brought back two donut shapes that clunked on the table. Lifting his white robe, Ajadu modeled two more donuts already fastened around the base of his birdlike legs. The heavy donuts easily hinged into C-shapes that snapped around Daniel's ankles like weights used by divers. Apparently, they'd be swimming to Jheean along the sea floor.

Ajadu downed the last of his jurg and tossed the empty bottle into a receptacle. "Ready to go?"

Ready was a loaded question. The coil technology was likely an apparatus for breathing underwater but razorfins might be another matter. "Ready, but I'll let you know if the route becomes intolerable."

The first step outside was a shocking reminder of the heat he'd already suffered, now even hotter. Daniel's thermal jacket kicked into high cool.

Ajadu locked up, then led straight across the beach. Tozz hopped behind, oblivious to the scorching sun but careful not to kick up sand. They waded into small waves. Daniel felt a prickle where the coils touched the back of his neck. Ankle weights slowed his steps, but the smooth sandy bottom allowed for an easy shuffle. Tozz was quickly over its head, apparently unconcerned about shorting out, though it might need another polymer rubdown after this excursion.

As Daniel ventured deeper, the sea water at his knees depressed into a bowl shape that expanded with each step. Ahead, Ajadu was already up to his shoulders with a curving shield of air surrounding him to keep the water at bay. Only his feet and the hem of his robe got wet.

Daniel's pants were soaked below the knee, but a cucumber-shaped bubble surrounded his upper body and formed a cap above his head as his body submerged.

Not bad. Better than scuba gear.

The enclosed bubble probably had enough air to last fifteen or twenty minutes, and if this retro steampunk technology failed, he could always release the ankle weights and swim to the surface.

Sand swirled along the sea bottom with each step. Bright sunlight filtered through turquoise water, reflecting off thousands of tiny sea creatures, each no bigger than a sewing needle. The thin worms sparkled as they twisted in corkscrew motions.

"Quite beautiful," Daniel said.

Ahead, Ajadu nodded, Daniel's voice having adequately transmitted the short distance through water.

Further on, a field of purple kelp sprouted from the seafloor, their long leaves nearly reaching to the surface, now about five meters overhead. "Interesting that so many of the plants here are purple."

Ajadu threaded a path through the kelp pods. "What other color would they be?"

"Green on my planet. Chlorophyll instead of retinal."

Ajadu grunted. "For two seasons, my grandfather and I surveyed many worlds in this sector. Prospecting often requires clearing vegetation. I have seen flowers of yellow, orange, red, and white. Living sticks that are brown or black. But I have never seen a green plant. Your home world sounds exotic."

It was a fascinating answer, scientifically. Daniel could easily imagine a planet like Bektash where chlorophyll didn't exist, but how many others were like it? An in-depth discussion of exobotany – accompanied by another round of jurg – would make for a pleasant afternoon.

But not today. There were more important goals just now. Nala was waiting somewhere in Jheean. Probably worried sick.

Ahead, a white oval doorway rose from the sea floor, oddly out of place. A portal – if such technology could exist underwater. Several large fish swam in circles, as big as any shark but with twin dorsal fins that gave them a modern jet-fighter look.

Ajadu paused and kept his voice low. "Be careful not to disturb the razorfins. They are hunters but also curious. They've seen the portal in action. Maybe they want to try it out."

One of the five-meter beasts swam through the center of the portal, coming out the other side with no ill effects. Its fins peaked at sharp tips – razor was the right descriptor. Daniel wasn't anxious to see if the creatures had teeth to match.

"Where does it go?"

"A backdoor," Ajadu replied. "The Jheean citadel has six corridors, each a different environment. This portal connects to the seawater corridor, but from there we can easily cross to the oxygen corridor – assuming no one stops us."

"Jheean security doesn't know about this portal?"

Ajadu shrugged and asked Tozz. "Do you?"

"Portal Bektash 61," Tozz answered, it's high-pitched voice somewhat garbled in the water. "Permitted."

"Permitted, your bot says. Not quite authorized but tolerated. Some of the diplomats of the Jheean seawater corridor enjoy discreet outings to the Bektash ocean. Diplomats have certain immunities. But, as for our use of this portal." He rapped Tozz on the head. "Forget we were ever here."

"Memory marked for erasure." Tozz squeaked.

"Good."

Apparently being a mechanic who sometimes serviced ailing s-bots carried with it some influence over security protocols.

They approached the portal carefully, Ajadu shooing the razorfins away. The big fish darted with each wave of his arm, but circled back again, either curious or hungry. A control panel on one side sported a series of tiny buttons. As Ajadu configured the device, Daniel did his best as backup shooer. The razorfins twitched each time he waved, but ominously kept their dark eyes fixed on Daniel's arm.

A light flickered on and a silver sheen spread through the interior of the portal, transforming the doorway into a mirror that perfectly reflected the seafloor surroundings. The razorfins became agitated. Their formation tightened.

Without prompting, Tozz stepped through. The mirror's surface wobbled and the s-bot simply disappeared. No transfer chairs, no hoods with yellow flashes. Ajadu offered for Daniel to go next.

Daniel hesitated. The jump might be only a few kilometers, but if compressed space were involved, a temporal offset would still be required.

"It won't kill you," Ajadu said, apparently aware of his concern. "Internal portals use a more advanced science. Suitable for shorter distances and gentler for species that cannot tolerate dimensional distortions. Just walk."

It seemed his only option to return to Jheean. If Nala were here, a few probing questions about portal physics would have made Daniel feel better, but then impulsive Nala would probably just step through. It had been hours since their separation. Finally, he had a path that would return him to their starting point. He'd find his wife and either get on with their mission or go home.

Or investigate this beacon of Ajadu's? If the visions were glimpses of the future, this last option seemed most likely. Almost destined.

Daniel took a deep breath and stepped forward. The seafloor, the razorfins, and Ajadu disappeared.

****

The world upended. Daniel existed but not within reality. He saw and heard, but not with senses.

He was inside a dark cave – or perhaps an expansive auditorium, though limited lighting made it impossible to determine its extent. Multiple glowing balls hovered in the air, some small, some larger. Each ball encapsulated a specific scene of reality outside this chamber.

Another hallucination. This one was as peculiar, and as unwelcome, as the hallucination at the beach.

A giant emerged from the darkness, at least three times Daniel's height. Thin. Bony. Alive. The giant brushed a long arm across several of the glowing balls, adjusting their encapsulated scenes in an intellectual task so complex that Daniel's mind spun trying to comprehend.

What are you doing? Daniel asked in pure thought.

The giant said nothing. Its complex actions warped the time and space represented inside each ball, forming new realities that were both artificial and temporary, like an artist drafting a quick sketch that might be accepted or tossed into the trash.

The result of the giant's abstract manipulations formed a series of vignettes within the balls – small snippets of designed reality where characters acted out hypothetical scenes. Daniel even recognized the players.

In one scene, individuals from multiple species filled a large room. Secretary General Nikolaus Jensen spoke in a clear but sorrowful voice, asking, "Humans are rejected?"

In another that hit frighteningly close to home, Daniel rose from a chair as Nala walked through the front door of their Santa Fe house. She dropped a car key fob on the entryway table. Her face was ashen, her voice shaky and tinged with frustration. "They've shut the whole program down. All of it."

In a third, Zin bowed to an agitated audience of humans, said goodbye, then stepped through a NASA portal for the last time. High-level officials included the US president. "We were so close," the president said.

The encapsulated vignettes projected a profound feeling of loss. Loss of knowledge and of participation. A loss to humanity, but a personal loss too.

Daniel observed without full comprehension but with a sick feeling that the floating balls told stories of events to come. Potential outcomes influenced by the giant's effort. In complex ways, the giant seemed to be undercutting human progress. Destabilizing fragile coalitions. Creating chaos.

Daniel spoke once more in his thought-voice. *Why are you doing this?*

The giant paused but gave no answer, disregarding Daniel's presence in this hyperreality of spacetime much as a busy executive ignores an intruding janitor.

The giant and the glowing balls faded to black leaving Daniel wondering what part he played in the depressing scenes. Was he a witness with no influence? Or could he oppose the giant's godlike manipulation of events? He had the distinct feeling that opportunities for prevention were closing rapidly.

****

Daniel blinked.

He was still underwater and still surrounded by a bubble of air. His feet were now on a solid floor instead of sand. Behind, a white portal reflected like a mirror. To one side, Tozz stood erect, its black eyes glossy and featureless. Behind the bot, a ramp led upward to a rippled surface about five meters overhead.

The bubble of air around him tasted stale with each breath. A concern of suffocation calmed when Ajadu stepped through the mirrored portal.

"You did well," Ajadu said.

"Not as well as you might think. Something happened – another hallucination. Just now, as I stepped through the portal, and it wasn't a happy scene." This time he couldn't attribute the delirium to heatstroke.

Ajadu paused. His narrow eyes squinted further. "Are we in danger?"

"Maybe not you and me, but I'm less sure about my people back on Earth. It feels like someone is working against us."

Ajadu absorbed the newest revelation without question. "Portals affect each species differently and could be the trigger of your vision. I have contacts who will know what to do, but I suggest we hurry." He pointed up the ramp.

As Daniel climbed, the air bubble dissolved as mysteriously as it had formed. He took in a breath. Chilled air, oxygenated. He switched his jacket back to warming mode. "This is Jheean?"

"Yes, the terminus of the seawater corridor," Ajadu said, shaking off the drips from the bottom of his white robe. They continued up the ramp which switch-backed once then deposited them in a rectangular all-glass enclosure.

To their left, members of various species passed beneath the enclosure. None took notice of the backdoor interlopers over their heads. "The oxygen corridor."

At the far end, a second ramp led down to the corridor. Their perch formed a quiet loft above the busy main avenue as well as a dike between the oxygenated air environment ahead and the seawater behind.

Daniel unstrapped the wire coil from his neck and handed it to Ajadu who stored them both in a robe pocket. Relief came with it. "I can't thank you enough. I wouldn't have made it on my own."

"My duty and my pleasure. But there is more we must accomplish, visionary. Come." He set off across the glass floor.

Before Daniel could take a step, Tozz squealed from behind. An arc of brilliant white plasma shot out from its forearms, creating a glowing rope that wrapped around Daniel's body and bound both arms to his sides.

Daniel jerked at the mild electric shock he'd felt once before. "What the hell?"

The s-bot's forearms touched, sealing a circular line of wobbling plasma around Daniel. It popped and sparked with electricity. The binding was tight and uncomfortable, but it didn't burn. Daniel twisted and stretched but couldn't break the bond.

Ajadu pivoted, his robes swirling. He shouted, "What is the purpose of this apprehension?"

"Security protocol," Tozz squeaked. "Protocol 422. Stand by."

"What?" The old birdman launched into a tirade in his native language while Tozz squealed responses back.

Daniel struggled against the binding. There was little chance of escape, but the s-bot's change of heart bothered him more. For reasons he couldn't fathom, Tozz had returned to its former role as a security officer. Why? Had the boundaries of Jheean triggered it? The portal? Or something else?

"Foolish bot." Ajadu turned to Daniel. "I should have disabled its higher cognitive functions when I had the chance. The s-bot has invoked an obscure security protocol. I have no idea why, but I will need diplomatic help to free you. Stay here. I will return shortly."

Daniel grimaced through clenched teeth. "Guess I don't have much choice."

Ajadu raised the hood on his robe and disappeared down the ramp and into the busy main corridor. No one in the crowd below seemed to notice the human above them, bound by an electric lasso. The glass might be transparent in only one direction.

Daniel eyed his captor. If this bot really did have higher level cognitive functions, reasoning might help.

"I thought we were past this, Tozz?"

The arc around Daniel's waist popped and sizzled, but Tozz remained silent.

"We teamed up. You helped me survive outside. I got the sand out of your joints. We did the Bektash desert trek together. Remember?"

"Desert," Tozz repeated, almost a whisper.

"Right. So, why don't you just release this binding, and I'll explain to the higher ups. Hell, I'm on a first name basis with Core and that's as high as you can go. You'll get a commendation for heroism. That's got to be worth something. Some time off? More polymer spray for your joints?"

"Polymer," Tozz repeated.

"It's not the *Tozz* thing, is it?"

"Not protocol."

"You're right, it's definitely not protocol, and protocol is important to you. I get it, and I apologize. You're Three One Zero Zero, heroic s-bot of the Bektash desert."

The s-bot lowered its forearms, loosening the plasma rope slightly. "Daniel Rice, human. Three One Zero Zero, s-bot." It paused. "Tozz acceptable."

This bot might not be self-aware, but it wasn't just a series of protocols strung together. There was a level of AI lurking inside that metallic grasshopper head, smart enough to figure out the origin of the moniker Daniel had given it. "So... are we still friends?"

Before the bot could answer, an upright centipede as big as a human appeared on the far side of the room. It wore a dark helmet over its front end. Tozz straightened up, tightening the plasma rope further. The centipede-person stopped and balanced on numerous umbrella fans that opened at its base. Several more fans popped out near its head.

The being issued a complex symphony of airy whistles and shushes. Tozz stared at the centipede, its head twitching left and right. More shushes erupted from the dark helmet.

The s-bot glanced to the ramp behind – the one leading back to seawater – then to Daniel. "Not protocol."

Daniel's eye was also drawn to the ramp. If the centipede expected Tozz to escort Daniel back to the underwater portal, the high-voltage arc around his waist was going to be an issue. Even if Tozz released the electric restraint, Daniel wasn't keen on a voluntary return to the Bektash desert. And it wasn't just the heat. Ajadu had taken Daniel's air bubble coil, and razorfins lurked on the other side.

The centipede's upper fans grew agitated, opening and closing with snapping sounds. Its next set of airy whistles were louder and punctuated by staccato puffs.

Daniel used his only free limb and tapped the bot with the toe of his shoe. "How about we just ignore this jerk and move on. You're the police officer here, not him."

The helmeted centipede leaped at Daniel, its fans flying and shushes shrieking. The verbal onslaught was accompanied by spittle that flicked across Daniel's face. The creature turned to Tozz and unleashed the same attack.

In a fair fight, Daniel could take him and would do it without hesitation. Tired of depressing visions and secret opponents, if a fistfight would get past these gatekeepers maybe it was time to shed the inquisitive scientist persona and become Daniel the Centipede Slayer. He balled up his fists.

"Come on, Tozz. We don't have to take this abuse. Turn off the electricity and let me at this guy." But instead of release, the plasma arc tightened further around Daniel's waist.

Tozz pivoted toward the ramp, issued an almost inaudible squeak, then started down, dragging Daniel toward the water.

11 REUNION

NALA STARED INTO the steep chute to the outside world feeling like she was peering into a chimney where a fire still burned. It hurt to think of Daniel out there.

Zin inched his way down the chute by pressing arms against opposite walls. When he reached the bottom, he stuck his head into the bright sunlight and called back up. "Bones, but no sign of Dr. Rice."

It had only been a few hours; most likely the remains of some previous ejectee. Zin yelled out Daniel's full name – doctor included – listened, then looked up at Nala with as distraught an expression as any android could muster. "I'm sorry, Dr. Pasquier. I'll jump to the sand. Perhaps if I search the perimeter, I'll find him."

"Wait!" Standing beside Nala, Theesah-ma busily scrolled through information that hung in the air above her spherical communications device. "The missing security token has reported a new position. The coordinates are within the Jheean citadel."

Nala tensed. "Daniel's token is back inside?"

"Yes. At the seawater corridor."

A token wasn't the same as the person who carried it. Could she allow herself elation at the news? Or was it a false alarm? Nala took the first step toward hope. "How far away?"

Theesah-ma's tongue-like head curled into that alien smile she did so well. "Very close, my dear. Shall I lead?"

Nala hugged the thin giant, then called down to Zin who was already clambering up. The android poked his head out of the disposal chute like a dumpster diver surfacing for air. "Dr. Rice has returned?"

"Hope so." Nala grabbed Zin's arm and pulled him out. "But let's get there before we lose him again."

****

Daniel dug his heels, but with thick hind legs and an inclined ramp Tozz had considerable leverage. There wasn't any rail to grab, which probably didn't matter since Daniel couldn't free his arms from the sparking electric arc that bound him like Wonder Woman's lasso. Why Tozz had turned on him was still unclear, but the centipede creature appeared to be in charge.

Daniel yelled, but there was no one else around to help. The helmeted centipede repositioned itself at the top of the ramp, a good spot to monitor the prisoner's execution.

Seawater – and Daniel's certain electrocution – was only a few feet away. Tozz stepped to the water's edge, stopped, and turned around. The plasma arc sizzled with high voltage.

Daniel stared into the glassy black eyes and forced a smile. "What do you say, buddy? You know I'll die if you drag me in there. Come on, there's got to be another way."

Tozz stopped pulling and stared back at Daniel. Its head jerked to the side several times. The centipede shushed loudly from the top of the ramp.

Tozz twitched. Its voice dropped an octave. "Protocol substitution. Destruct sequence. One. Code one. One A. Execute on three, two, one..."

With a pop, the plasma arc disappeared, freeing Daniel's arms once more. Now, a ring of blue-white light encircled Tozz's head, reverberating with a buzzing sound that crescendoed in pitch.

BANG.

Tozz's head propelled upward along a central shaft, separating from its body until wires snapped taut, leaving the decapitated head dangling from the end of the shaft. A ring of smoke drifted through the air as if a cannon had fired.

Daniel's gaze alternated between the remains of the s-bot and the centipede. For its part, the cause of the havoc stood frozen, clearly uncertain how or why the bot had self-destructed.

Daniel brushed a hand against the lifeless head that now hung limp from wires. His fingers squeezed into fists, and Daniel turned cold eyes to the loathsome creature at the top of the ramp.

His voice shook. "You did this."

Daniel bolted up the ramp. He slammed into the helmeted centipede, knocking it backwards. The creature shrieked an airy scream, righted itself, then slashed back at Daniel with its upper fans. The fan edges – sharp as a yucca's blade – cut through the arm of Daniel's jacket and drew blood.

He ignored the sting, landing several punches into meaty areas and denting the creature's helmet. More shrieks. The centipede fled across the glass floor and down the far ramp with Daniel in hot pursuit.

The ramp led down to a smaller chamber where another portal stood, matching the seawater portal Daniel had just passed through. A mirror materialized within its interior and the centipede jumped through, disappearing in a blink. Daniel skidded to a stop, not daring to follow to who-knows-where.

His breathing steadied. His fists unclenched even as his heart still raced. "That s-bot was my friend," he growled.

There was no one to hear it. The chamber seemed to be no more than an arrival-departure gate for the portal and an overhead passageway to the seawater petal of the Jheean flower.

Daniel stared at the portal's mirrored surface for another minute. No sounds. No wavering. The centipede was gone.

Daniel left the chamber to rejoin the citizens of Jheean going about their routine in the oxygen corridor. No one seemed to notice the angry human. The fighter within him faded. Logic returned.

Find someone with a sphere hovering at their shoulder.

The device would no doubt connect him to others, possibly Ajadu or even Zin. And from there, Nala. He wouldn't rest until she was back in his arms.

Jheean's central avenue stretched ahead. Behind, a black wall rose at least thirty meters high. What had looked like clear glass from the inside of the loft now appeared as dark stone, a curious effect of material science that Daniel had no time to understand.

The broad avenue and its marketplaces were familiar – he'd been here before, just further down. At its far end would be a landing area, a gold capsule, and a five-mile tube to a glass cocoon with a portal that could return Daniel to Earth. But that option could wait too. He wouldn't be going home without Nala.

Vendor stalls filled the avenue's center with a variety of creatures selling their wares. A few stared. Most ignored the human passing through their market. S-bots might still be among these citizens; he'd need to be careful.

Tozz had given its life for Daniel. Though labeled low intelligence by Zin, this s-bot certainly had value beyond a security agent. Daniel could think of a few humans who'd done less with their lives. Tozz had analyzed conflicting commands, searched for a protocol that could provide resolution, and found one. Self-destruction. Tozz would get a posthumous commendation if Daniel had anything to say about it.

Daniel stopped. Not far ahead, a human figure emerged from the kaleidoscope of aliens. His heart leaped.

"Nala!"

They ran to each other, and Daniel lifted her off the ground in a long-overdue embrace.

Nala buried her face in Daniel's shoulder, sobbing. "I thought I'd never find you. I'm so sorry, Daniel. I shouldn't have jumped."

It seemed like days since they'd leaped into the mega-slide. Daniel brushed against her cheek, luxuriating as her hair fell around his face. He inhaled deeply, filling his senses with her.

"Tough day," he whispered in her ear. "But not your fault. I'm back and still in one piece. I got some help." Tozz's demise weighed heavily on his mind. Ajadu might be risking his own neck at this very minute, but Nala was back. As far as Daniel was concerned, they'd never separate again.

Nala began to ask for details, but Daniel held a finger to her lips, distracted by a towering figure that loomed behind her. A gaunt biped on lanky legs stepped closer. Except for a swirling red dress that covered its midsection, he recognized its form. He'd seen it before.

The giant from Daniel's hallucination had suddenly become very real. He pointed almost straight up. "Who is that?"

Nala must have heard the concern in his voice, whispering, "Don't worry, she's nice."

"Theesah-ma," the giant cooed. He'd heard the soft voice before, too.

Zin emerged from behind the giant. "Dr. Rice, I'm so happy to see you again. Theesah-ma is a Litian-nolo representative. Exactly the person you need to see."

A Litian-nolo. There was hope for this disaster of a mission.

Maybe.

Daniel gazed up at the lanky creature. Bony, knobby joints. A funny, flat head with green eyes. Zin had given only the barest of details of Litian-nolos, and none had involved their appearance. Litian-nolos were time mentors with knowledge of the affliction Zin had called entanglement.

Zin had never mentioned their size. Or the soft, soothing voice. In Daniel's latest vision, this giant had been busy creating a frustrating future for humans. Perhaps Zin wasn't aware about that aspect of Litian-nolos. Nala seemed to think this one was friendly.

The giant folded in ways no human knees could, eventually compressing to one-fourth her original size. She held out an arm with suction cups along its tip.

"So wonderful to meet Nala's Daniel." Her voice was smooth as butter, gentle, and friendly. She'd make a good GPS guide.

Maybe Nala was right about the amicable nature of this alien, but Daniel remained wary of her intent. He took the alien hand in his. "I have a strange feeling we've met before."

"How interesting," Theesah-ma said. "No, we have not. But I understand why you say this. You are an instigator, lovely Daniel."

Lovely and *instigator* weren't words commonly put in the same sentence. Daniel whispered to Nala. "You want to catch me up a little here?"

"Theesah-ma has it figured out," Nala whispered back. "She agrees with Zin, you're entangled with one of their time mentors. Don't ask me how any of this works. She knows."

Zin, his hearing sharp as ever, nodded his agreement of their whispers. Two opinions Daniel trusted had indicated Theesah-ma would be helpful. He set aside his skepticism. For now.

"I'm entangled?"

"You are," Theesah-ma cooed. "And in danger, dear Daniel. I tried to prevent you from entering Jheean."

"You sent the bot?"

"Yes."

Daniel didn't know whether to thank her or start another fight. The confusion between friend and foe in this complex world was getting hard to sort out.

"I was thrown outside. And somebody tossed the s-bot after me. The bot is dead now, by the way. Self-destructed to save my life."

Daniel related the story of his ejection and trek across the desert. Nala pulled him tighter as his descriptions of heat and thirst escalated. When he got to the part about meeting Ajadu, Zin interrupted.

"Ajadu the Colonist contacted me only moments ago. He will meet us at the Oxygen Loft."

Daniel pointed down the hallway behind him. "I was just there, I think. Had a fight with a spitting bug."

"A Torak?" Zin asked.

"Maybe so." Daniel relayed the second part of his story including how the helmeted centipede had escaped through a mirrored portal.

With a wave of his metal arm, Zin led the group to the avenue's end and a rendezvous with Ajadu. They climbed the side ramp to the loft. No sign of Ajadu, but the connection to the seawater sector was still blocked by the pitiful remains of Tozz.

Nala stroked the mangled head of the metal grasshopper. "Poor guy."

Zin stood erect, his metal hands folded together, his head bowed. Put a stovepipe hat on him and he'd make a good funeral director. "I will arrange for this bot's cleanup."

Daniel wondered where the other hero in this story had gone. A scan down the avenue – once more visible from inside the glass loft – didn't turn up anyone dressed in white robes.

"Any word from Ajadu?"

Zin answered. "None. I have sent two position report requests in the past minute, both returned with a request denied code. Position cloaking is within Ajadu's right, but odd considering he wishes to reconnect with you. Colonists are a curious people."

Theesah-ma's head curled at the edges. "They are, indeed. Mythologists with a tenuous connection to reality."

Daniel interjected. "I admit Ajadu's story of the Ancients sounds like folklore, but he says the Star Beacon is a real place."

Theesah-ma had already folded to human height in the more restricted space of the loft. She cozied up to Daniel, even taking his hand. Her soothing voice made every word sound reassuring. "Lovely Daniel. Thank your friend for his help. Ajadu most certainly saved you from grief in the Bektash desert. But accept his stories for what they are – a fantasy that serves the interests of Colonists. Yes, the Star Beacon is a real place. A historical site honored by all. Built by a people lost to the winds of time. No one knows who the Ancients were or where they went. Colonists claim kinship. But there are good reasons to doubt this claim."

"Very true," Zin said. "The Five Season Conflict, for one."

Daniel was about to ask for an explanation when a white robed figure strode across the loft's glass floor. The hem of his robe was still damp.

"Ajadu," Daniel embraced the birdman as though they were old friends. In some ways, they were. "As you can see, I'm free." He motioned over his shoulder to the battered s-bot.

Ajadu nodded, apparently recognizing s-bot self-destruction. His hovering sphere flashed a green beam to the corresponding sphere floating at Theesah-ma's shoulder, each device making a clicking sound.

"Theesah-ma," Ajadu said, bowing his hooded head.

"Ajadu," the giant responded. "Most welcome to Jheean. Do you still operate your desert establishment by the sea?"

"The Wreck, such as it is. There are fewer Colonists in the Bektash desert these days." Ajadu lowered his hood exposing his bony head with protruding beak. His words to Theesah-ma were blunt. "Are you here to help Daniel? Or stop him?"

Theesah-ma's green eyes blinked in a rolling slow motion. The electronic attachment on her face made breathing sounds, but the giant gave no answer.

Ajadu turned to Daniel. "You must hurry, my friend. If Theesah-ma will not take you to the Star Beacon, I will do it myself. But any alteration from the specifics of your vision could make things worse. I am not a part of your vision. She is."

Rising to half-height, Theesah-ma towered over the Colonist. "Talk of visions is nonsense. Daniel is an entangled instigator. The complexities of this science are great. A Colonist would not understand."

107

"Arrogant as always." Ajadu pulled on Daniel's arm. "Your vision is real. You know this and so do I. Follow its power. Go to the Star Beacon. Fulfill your destiny and that of your people too."

Vision. Entanglement. Two words for the same thing?

Science had always stood in opposition to mysticism but sometimes shared the same origin. Constellations were a good example. Mystics believed star patterns in the sky had influence over people's lives, but astronomers had adopted the same patterns as convenient frames of reference. There was no reason for any scientist to be elitist. Uncovering reality had always been the core principle behind science – even when the starting point derived from the realm of mystics.

With Ajadu on one arm, and Nala on the other, Daniel's eyes turned up to Theesah-ma. "Ajadu has a point. If the Star Beacon is real, I need to see it. I already have some thoughts about it. We humans tend to be curious about things we don't understand. We form theories, then search for evidence."

Daniel wasn't quite ready to disclose his still-forming Star Beacon theory; there would be time for that later. "But before we go anywhere, if this entanglement phenomenon is real, I need to understand it."

12 ENTANGLED

"I WILL EXPLAIN what I can," Theesah-ma told Daniel. "But I am not a time mentor. Time entanglement is complex. A science studied by Litian-nolos for generations. Some say we are masters. But a time mentor will tell you such mastery is impossible."

She reached out with knobby arms and took Daniel's hands. "But first, please tell me of these *visions*." She emphasized the last word with the skepticism of a parent addressing their child's imaginary playmate.

Vision. Dream. Premonition. Daniel wished for a more scientific vocabulary. "Dreams back on Earth. But there were two more here. Different. Maybe hallucinations, I'm not sure. My dreams on Earth started with someone calling me to come here. Was it you?"

"A common mistake," Theesah-ma diagnosed. "Some feel compelled. Some call it a duty. But no one is calling. Not even Hataki-ka, a Litian-nolo time mentor who wisely advised me to intercept you. It is the entanglement that compels you. Nothing else." She pulled on his hand. "Please, go on."

Daniel continued with the delirium he'd experienced in the desert. He explained the odd feeling of floating in space, the gentle voice – Theesah-ma's voice, he believed. A large disc of glass with beveled edges and a red laser that flashed across a star-filled sky. Theesah-ma nodded as he talked but said nothing.

Daniel was careful about the second hallucination, pointing out that although he was certain the being who crafted events of the future was a Litian-nolo, he couldn't say for certain it was Theesah-ma. As he explained, he realized that he'd fallen into the age-old trap of "they all look the same to me". Its racist origins applied equally to alien species.

Nala hung tight on Daniel's arm as he spoke. Theesah-ma absorbed the story in silence, her large green eyes closing at times.

When he was finished, Theesah-ma offered her own interpretation. "Not visions. But not hallucinations either. Ajadu was right in advising you to seek help."

The birdman hadn't given that specific advice, but Theesah-ma seemed to be offering an olive branch to the Colonist. Ajadu, his hood pulled over his head once more, leaned against the glass wall of the loft, paying more attention to the activity in the Jheean corridor below.

Theesah-ma lowered her voice. "An inflection point is coming."

Nala winced. She'd clearly heard this pronouncement before.

Theesah-ma explained. "Litian-nolo time mentors have seen it. And, lovely Daniel, you have seen it too. But due to inexperience, you misinterpret it."

Daniel didn't mind the snub. His curiosity was off the charts. Finally, there was someone to explain these dreams, these hallucinations – this entanglement.

Theesah-ma continued. "I have studied humans. I have read about you, Daniel Rice. You are a time traveler, are you not?"

"Once. Thirty years into our future."

Technically, there had been three forward jumps. The first to 2053, but from there he'd leaped all the way to the twenty-fifth century to save his own skin. Then once more to 2053 to save Jacquelyn – Jackie Jetson, as Nala had named her.

"Even one transition through time is enough. You are entangled."

He glanced to Zin, who often hung in the background for discussions like this. "That's what Zin told me. What did you call it, officially?"

110

Zin stepped forward. "Entanglement of conscious experience across the multiple probability pathways of a multiverse."

Daniel turned back to Theesah-ma. "That?"

The giant nodded. "Zin describes it well. Any fundamental particle of our universe can become entangled. An electron. A photon. Time is quantized too."

"A chronon," Nala added.

"Yes. I am so glad humans understand this science," Theesah-ma said.

Nala shrugged. "Well, we're learning."

"Likewise, Litian-nolos cannot claim complete understanding. But we try. Far better to be a student of science than a denier." She motioned toward Ajadu who remained alone, staring out beyond the glass.

"We humans have our deniers, too," Nala added. "But the rest of us do our best to drag them forward, sometimes kicking and screaming."

Daniel had always been a skeptic but tried not to be a denier, especially when the scientific principle was new. "You're saying my conscious experience is entangled across multiverse timelines?"

"Yes. A connection forms within the time traveler's mind. It can be beneficial but also dangerous." She leaned close to Daniel. "Like our time mentors, you are experiencing memories of alternate futures."

Memories of the future.

Nonsensical, but Daniel had already seen the illogic of time travel firsthand. It wasn't hard to grasp this newest concept. "A year ago, I jumped to the future, but when I returned, we took steps to erase every part of that future – and I believe we succeeded. Yet, I still retain those future events in my memory. They feel just as real as any past event, even though they exist only on an alternate timeline that has now vanished."

"Perhaps vanished. Perhaps not. Time manipulation leads to uncertainties. Alternate timelines must be continuously managed. This is the work of time mentors, work you have witnessed in your future memory – your hallucination, as you call it. But, lovely Daniel, you understand so little. You are not yet even an apprentice. To become a time mentor can take a lifetime.

"Hataki-ka cautioned me of the coming inflection. He believes you could upset a delicate balance. He calls you a rogue. As I explained to your Nala, Litian-nolos are not of one mind. While I see the promise in your species, Hataki-ka sees only the ignorance and wars."

Daniel rubbed his temples in a feeble attempt to relieve growing stress. He'd be the first to admit human ignorance. Scientific illiteracy was high. A third of humans had no understanding of evolution. When quizzed, twenty percent weren't sure if the Earth was round.

His own ignorance of time manipulation was now on display. No doubt he had much to learn, but if timeline adjustments required maintenance then even the altered 2053 future might not stay *fixed*. Daniel wasn't anxious to have any more battles with Father, the preacher who had planned a dystopian society but was now in a prison cell.

Theesah-ma's explanation – though beyond fantastic – had a ring of truth. Alternate timelines required ongoing management. Humans might need to employ their own time mentors.

Please, not me.

Daniel sighed. He'd been dragged into service before. Skillful politicians could be very persuasive. He pulled Nala closer. Wherever this was leading, he wasn't planning on letting her out of his sight.

Nala seemed to be on the same wavelength. "Surely, there's a way to break Daniel's chronon entanglement. In the lab, we disrupt entangled particles all the time. That's what decoherence is all about."

Theesah-ma cooed softly. "Lovely Nala do not despair for your Daniel. There is comfort. Entanglement can be managed. Others have been successful. Perhaps Daniel can meet with our time mentors. They know more than I."

Daniel and Nala nodded to each other. Progress toward ending his affliction. But it seemed there were more immediate concerns. "You said an inflection point is coming. Ajadu believes the Star Beacon is involved. I agree. I don't yet know why, but I need to go there. You do too."

Theesah-ma thought for a moment. "I worry for your safety. As yet, you have no skills. You cannot know what will happen at an inflection point. It may be better to let others manage."

Others had already done enough damage. Daniel had been nearly killed by desert heat and electrocution. So far, the centipede – and whoever else might be involved – had gotten away with it. He wasn't about to leave the human impact of this inflection point in the hands of a Litian-nolo time mentor he'd never met.

There were three other advisors in the room. "Zin? What do you think?"

Zin nodded. "Theesah-ma is correct, Dr. Rice. Though I should add that when probabilities are involved, the inflection point could turn out to be beneficial."

"Ajadu?"

The old birdman turned to face Daniel. "I believe your people and mine are linked. You must go. It is your destiny. And my duty."

Daniel had never accepted the concept of destiny or fate, but Colonists were storytellers. They might use different words for what a human might call curiosity. Daniel would never restrain his curiosity. It's what drove him.

Nala would get the final say. He locked eyes with her, and she gave a reassuring nod. They might still be newlyweds, but their communication had already become heart-to-heart. Words weren't required.

Daniel returned to Theesah-ma. "We're going. At least Nala and I. Will you come with us?"

Nala pulled on Theesah-ma's arm. "Please. Show us around. Tell us what you know. If Daniel's future memory is any indication, you're supposed to be there."

The giant closed her eyes like she was trying to see that future too. "Perhaps."

"Come on, TM," Nala pressed. "You said yourself that humans are smarter than you thought. We're a lot more than just *lovely*. Hell, you haven't even seen Daniel in action yet. He does things that will blow you away. You don't want us to be like the Sandzvallons, do you? Shunned. Always in the dark until we destroy ourselves."

Theesah-ma was silent for a moment. "Very well. Dear Nala, lovely Daniel. I shall take you to the Star Beacon."

Nala hugged the bony giant. For two fundamentally different species, they seemed as tight as sisters. But Nala made friends easily and celebrated the most unexpected friendships with a passion that Daniel would never muster if he lived to a hundred.

Ajadu bowed. "Then my duty is done."

"Not entirely," Zin said. "We could use your help in an investigation to determine the facts behind the s-bot destruction." Zin pointed to Tozz. "While you were discussing entanglement, I was in contact with Jheean security. Dr. Rice, the Torak you encountered is Chorl, an apprentice to Litian-nolo time mentor Hataki-ka. It is not yet clear why Chorl acted as it did or why the bot was compromised. S-bots are expected to follow strict protocols, which don't include killing visitors to Jheean."

"Not sure I'm liking this Hataki-ka guy," Nala said to Theesah-ma.

Theesah-ma's head quivered in an agitated way. She might have been wondering the same thing given that she'd already admitted Litian-nolos were not of one mind.

"Come," Theesah-ma said, gathering long arms around Daniel and Nala like a mother comforting her children. "We cannot know what has not yet happened."

After goodbyes to Zin and Ajadu, Theesah-ma guided Daniel and Nala down the ramp to the oxygen corridor stopping in front of the same portal where the Torak had disappeared.

Given the right configuration, there was no doubt the Star Beacon lay beyond – along with the infamous inflection point that would lead to branching timelines, some good, some bad – the frustrating vignettes he'd witnessed in his last hallucination, if Theesah-ma was correct. The next few minutes might require every one of Daniel's skills.

Theesah-ma shrank to the height of the doorway and touched configuration buttons on its side. A mirror sheen appeared, reflecting Daniel and Nala standing in front of it.

Daniel touched a finger to its surface causing the mirror to wobble. "The underwater portal was the same. No transfer chairs, you just walk through."

"You go first," Nala said. "But I'll be right behind. No more separations, okay?" Daniel agreed wholeheartedly.

Daniel's fingers slid through the mirror as though the glass was nothing more than an optical illusion. His body followed either from momentum or from Nala's gentle push. He stepped through from the ordinary to the exceptional. From reality to the uncharted. From three dimensions to four.

Daniel saw stars.

13 STARS

STARS. EVERYWHERE. By the thousands, up, down, in every direction. But one dominated, front and center. Blazing dull red like a glowing ember in a fireplace, this solar furnace was close enough to make out individual bubbles of plasma boiling across its surface. Yet somehow, Daniel was unscathed by its fiery surface.

He stared, dumbfounded by his impossible position next to this star and among uncountable more. The whole galaxy splayed across the sky with a billion pinpricks of light, filaments of darker dust, and pink splashes of hydrogen nebulae. He stood on something firm, yet there was nothing to see. He breathed, even within the vacuum of space.

The spectacle before him was enough to stir a deep reverence for the natural world, but it was accompanied by a feeling that he'd been here before. In one repeated dream that manifested again as a desert delirium, he'd floated in space with his feet touching nothing.

Theesah-ma might be right. His dreams weren't mystical premonitions, they were memories of future events but created out of order. Remembered first, then later formed from real events.

Events that will occur, or that might occur?

There was no way to know until the future played out. Multiple timelines in a probability multiverse had never meshed with common sense, but the universe was under no obligation to obey human logic. An entire branch of science – quantum physics – defied everyday sensibilities. Einstein's relativity wasn't any better.

Behind him, a mirrored doorway hovered in the void of space. Nala stepped through, her eyes widening as she absorbed the stunning view. Like his own, her feet touched nothing. Theesah-ma followed a second later and stood quietly next to the speechless humans.

As stars go, this one was relatively cool, a red dwarf in the last stages of its life. Like a campfire at night, its radiation was strong enough to warm cheeks but no more.

"Spectacular," Nala whispered. She looked straight down. No platform. No glass. Nothing but stars. "Where are we? What are we even standing on?"

Theesah-ma's voice soothed. "A generated field. As firm as any planetary surface. Do not fear."

There was no sensation of falling. Daniel took a small step forward, marveling at a green glow that appeared where his foot landed. The glow disappeared just as quickly as it formed. "Something surrounds us, or we wouldn't be alive."

"A torus," Theesah-ma replied. "An energy tube shaped like… a donut, humans might say. The red star is in the center. Shall I turn the footstep markers off? Some prefer the torus unseen."

Daniel stepped again and the green glow returned, briefly elongating into a curving directional arrow, then faded. "No, leave it on. It's steadying." The temporary glow outlined a path like a gymnast's balance beam with an infinite drop on either side. Yet there was something about the firmness of each step that overrode fears of falling.

"The torus continues all the way around the star?" Nala asked. The scale of the engineering was beginning to become apparent.

"In a way. The torus is a four-dimensional ring surrounding three-dimensional space. Lengths in our direction of travel are compressed. Our destination lies far ahead, but we will arrive quickly."

Nala took the lead, clearly interested to see what fantastic object might lie ahead. She stepped with care, following the green glow as it formed a curving path. Daniel followed, curious but wary.

Literally, living the dream.

As they moved, a solar prominence – a strand of burning plasma that leaped from the star's surface – swung into view. Dark spots appeared on the star's horizon and moved closer with each step. It was like walking around a solar model, yet the gentle heat confirmed this star was the real thing.

They ambled further, and the star rotated in synchronization; spatial compression was certainly in play. A few steps within this torus might correspond to millions of kilometers outside.

"It isn't like any 3-D compression I've managed," Nala said. "We're walking in a circle, so the direction keeps changing. How does compression work at all?" Ever the physicist, she was one step ahead of Daniel's thoughts, but her question made sense. Humans could compress 3-D space, but only in one direction selected in advance.

"Do you know differential calculus?" Theesah-ma asked. "A kind of mathematics."

"I couldn't be a physicist without it."

"Then you understand the tangent of a curve?"

The glowing green path curved ahead of Nala. It wasn't hard to imagine a complete circle around the star. "Well, in calculus terms, the tangent is a vector defined by the derivative at any point on a circle."

"Correct. And we walk a circle now."

"So, the torus compresses space using the derivative of the circle function?"

"Nala, you are as smart as you are beautiful. Differential compression was first invented by a Litian-nolo. We are very proud."

It was as clear an example as anyone could ask for – the whole reason to join Sagittarius Novus. Humans had only scratched the surface of math, science, engineering, and probably many other subjects only imagined.

"Please continue," the graceful giant said. "The best is yet to come."

Their steps were steadier now. A bulge developed at the star's horizon giving it a teardrop shape. More steps, and the teardrop stretched to a flaming ribbon of fire as if some unknown force were sucking the star's energy into space. At the tip of the elongated flare, a glittering object appeared, small and round with facets that caught the starlight and produced a spectrum of diffracted colors. It almost looked like a diamond.

They walked closer. The sparkling object grew larger, revealing a disc shape with beveled edges. Its jeweled facets sparkled white, red, and orange. From the disc's center, a brilliant beam of red blasted across the starry sky, its energy clearly drawn from the star and focused by this enormous disc of faceted glass. Daniel's heart beat faster as the familiar scene played out like a book cover that is finally realized within its pages.

They rounded the disc's edge. Its far side had been scooped out into a gracefully curving bowl and polished to perfection to reflect the countless millions of stars in the sky.

Nala stopped. Her mouth dropped open. "Holy crap, it's a mirror."

"A space telescope," Daniel said, stunned by its enormity. The giant mirror sprawled across a full third of the sky, blocking out the red dwarf behind it. Above its surface, several struts suspended a smaller mirror facing in the opposite direction, no doubt positioned precisely at the parabolic focal point.

The red laser threaded through holes in both the primary and secondary mirrors, then shot across the sky to split the starry background. Its brilliance diminished with distance, eventually disappearing altogether somewhere in the depths of space.

Vision realized.

Daniel had expected the "future memory" to come into existence, but the mirror's majestic size and the laser's brilliance had turned out to be more inspiring than he'd realized. It was like standing at the Eiffel Tower or the Taj Mahal. You've seen the photographs all your life, but now you're really there.

Nala craned her neck to the red streak. "Wow," she whispered. "The Star Beacon. Just as you described, Daniel."

Theesah-ma picked up her role as tour guide. "In human measures, the mirrored bowl is two hundred kilometers across. It can resolve planets more than a thousand light-years away."

By comparison, the James Webb telescope – the largest space telescope yet constructed by humans – was a mere six meters. The Star Beacon was thirty-thousand times larger, and ancient too.

Daniel shook his head. "What an achievement. I finally understand why everyone is so impressed. Ajadu said it's twenty-five million years old. Accurate?"

"An estimate," Theesah-ma confirmed. "It consumes the star's energy at a fixed rate, revealing its age. The Star Beacon was constructed before you. Before me. Before everyone at Jheean. We call its builders the Ancients, but we know little of them."

"It doesn't look that old," Nala said. "There's hardly a scratch on it."

"We are still at distance. Walk further."

They followed the curving path, bringing the enormous mirror close enough to blot out most of the stars. The invisible torus passed beneath struts that held the secondary mirror at the focal point, providing an immersive experience with a different view of the colossal structure in every direction. Up close, it was easy to see scattered pockmarks across the polished surface. Meteor strikes, most likely, a feature of any ancient surface. The struts were cracked in places, but still held together.

"Many scientists have studied this artifact and the considerable data saved in its recordings. The Star Beacon includes thrusters to reposition the mirror to any direction. It houses instruments that measure the chemistry of distant planets. Its beacon of light can be modulated to form coded messages. The Ancients built it not simply to study the stars. They searched for life. They hoped to communicate."

"But they failed?" Nala asked.

"Recorded data provides evidence of messages sent to many points in the sky. But no evidence of a single reply."

"Sad. It's such a magnificent device. The beacon is beautiful."

Theesah-ma's voice was silky smooth. "It draws the eye."

Daniel gasped as words came into existence precisely as he'd heard them. *It draws the eye.* Events – even specific words – were unfolding as predicted. As *remembered*, if Theesah-ma's explanation was correct. But what to do about it? If the Star Beacon had gone from future memory to reality, would the discouraging vignettes become just as real? Humans rejected from Sagittarius Novus, science programs cancelled back on Earth, and Zin parting ways with humans forever. In a multiverse, those events might be just around the corner. Or might never exist.

Theesah-ma opened her jointed arms in an embrace of the red beam stretching across a starry sky. "The Star Beacon is beautiful. And mysterious. The Ancients abandoned this instrument long ago. Nearly five million years, in your measures. In addition to the star consumption, we have analyzed meteorite impacts. The pockmarks you see on its surface. Microscopic particles orbiting this star strike with regularity. The angle of impact tells us this mirror has not moved since the people who built it disappeared."

Numbers had a way of lodging in Daniel's mind. "Four point eight million years ago, according to Tozz. The Colonists say that's when the Ancients split into two groups. The Great Divide, they call it. They even have a mark on their back to commemorate the event."

Theesah-ma folded her long arms into her compact form. "I am aware. Colonist genes have been studied. Indeed, their mark was engineered long ago. Millions of years? Perhaps, though genetic dating is inexact. Most members reject any connection to the Star Beacon. A coincidence, they say. Colonists are mythologists, not scientists or engineers. A relationship to the Ancients is unlikely."

She waved to the Star Beacon as proof that any descendant of the talented race who built this structure would rank higher than storytelling miners.

"Not sure I agree," Daniel said. "The passage of time can transform a civilization, and not always in a good way. We have lots of examples on Earth."

Theesah-ma was quiet for a moment, thinking. "Nothing is simple. The myth of the Great Divide. The mark on their backs. Their claim to a home planet they call Dissat. But where is this lost world? Their evidence is scant. A book. A map that leads nowhere. A few relics of jewelry. No more. We have scoured every system within a hundred light years and not found it. The beam itself points to nothing. Empty space."

Daniel had been wondering about that. The red laser did seem to be a pointer though what it was pointing to could be light years away.

"Dear Daniel, Colonists often neglect to tell the whole story. They claim the Star Beacon as their own. Before this torus was constructed, Colonists tried to seal off this space. They placed gunships and charged fees to anyone who wanted to visit. It was a source of much conflict, until Core stepped in."

There were always two sides to every story. Ajadu had neglected to mention gunships.

Nala joined in. "We've had similar issues on Earth over sacred ground. Hawaiians have long opposed the observatories at the top of Mauna Kea. Like the Colonists, Hawaiians are pretty vocal about it."

Daniel confirmed Nala's comment with a nod, and Theesah-ma continued. "The Star Beacon is historic. We all agree. But this ancient place cannot belong to one species. It is for all to study. Today, we include humans. It is your turn now. What interpretation will you assign to this masterpiece?"

Phrased that way, the mysteries surrounding the Star Beacon formed an irresistible challenge for any scientific investigator. Daniel was already hooked. For now, he set aside Ajadu's declaration of destiny and focused on the intellectual puzzle. Like humans, the Ancients had been searching for other life. And then they stopped. Why? Did they find what they were looking for? Theesah-ma had said the beacon pointed to nothing but empty space. A testable hypothesis.

Just to the beacon's left, a bright blue-white star stood out against the background of the Milky Way. "Just curious. It seems oriented toward the brightest star in the sky."

Theesah-ma looked up. "Bonda Jon. Some say it served as an alignment star."

She spoke in her own language, mellow words that caused the hovering sphere at her shoulder to flicker. In the sky a label appeared, floating next to the bright star. It was no doubt projected there by superb technology, but the heads-up display wasn't the primary attention grabber. The label read, *Rigel*.

"It seems humans have a name for Bonda Jon too."

Daniel smiled. With all the jumping through portals they could be almost anywhere, but now he had a known reference point. "Rigel is one of the brightest stars in our sky, too. About eight hundred light years away. Obviously, closer here." There were several other stars almost as bright. "Can your device label the others?"

Orientation was an important first step in any analysis and having established one point in common, Daniel's curiosity was soaring.

"Perhaps. The full breadth of human data is not yet integrated into the An Sath collection." Theesah-ma issued another command and more labels appeared.

To the right of the red beam, the label Betelgeuse popped up next to a bright orange star. More followed: Canopus, Saiph, Mintaka, Alnitak, Bellatrix, and others.

"Wow." Daniel swiveled in a circle, noting the star Alnilam directly behind them. He laughed along with Nala. "Unbelievable. We're deep inside Orion."

As seen from Earth, the constellation of Orion the Hunter was composed of three stars in a tight row, the "belt" stars of Alnitak, Alnilam, and Mintaka, along with four "body" stars, Betelgeuse and Bellatrix as the hunter's shoulders and Saiph and Rigel as the legs. Given that more distant Alnilam – the middle belt star – was directly behind, their position gave a literal feeling of being *inside* Orion.

Daniel searched the sky for a dim white star among the sea of lights. He'd never find it. Home was at least a thousand light years away, and Sol would be far too dim for human eyes to make out.

Nala seemed to understand too. "Can your device pinpoint Earth?"

Theesah-ma checked her sphere. "I should have come prepared. Newcomers to the Star Beacon enjoy finding their home system. Mine is there." She pointed to a tight grouping of stars. "What you call the Beehive Cluster. I shall try to locate yours. One moment."

A popup of alien text and colored lines appeared, and Theesah-ma pushed the endpoints of several lines in some complex calculation of geometries. "Yes. I have it now."

Overhead, four orange triangles popped into existence and flung across the sky like arrowheads to their target. The triangles settled at a noticeably empty spot in the sky, then gathered into a circle with their narrow ends pointing to its center. The triangles pulsated inward like a heartbeat, clearly drawing attention to the emptiness within the circle they'd formed.

Theesah-ma cooed, "My eyes cannot resolve your star. Can yours?"

"Not me," Nala said. "Earth is in that circle?"

"If my calculations are correct, yes."

The markers were about halfway between Rigel on the left and Betelgeuse on the right, evidence that supported her computed position. The insignificant yellow dwarf that humans called the sun was simply too far away to see.

Daniel followed the beacon's laser until it faded into the sea of stars and dust beyond Rigel. It certainly wasn't pointing to Earth, but it was the same general direction. Daniel's mind churned as multiple thoughts formed in rapid succession.

"Any chance your handy device can compute star positions over time?"

All stars move as the galaxy rotates, some stars only jostling a bit relative to their neighbors, others with trajectories based on gravitational encounters in the past. *Proper motion*, astronomers called it. For most stars, the position changes were too small to notice over a human lifetime.

But over millions of years…

Theesah-ma's flexible head curled. "Lovely Daniel, you ask what others before you have asked. How did this sky look almost five million years ago? When the torus was constructed, this question was built into its design. Watch."

Theesah-ma voiced an alien command different in style than her own language, a word that didn't sound much different than abracadabra.

Like magic, the starry sky began to shift. Rigel drifted higher. Mintaka moved further right, dimming as it went. Dozens of other stars drifted in various directions, including the four triangles that Theesah-ma's device had projected into empty space. The markers continued to pulsate as they moved left, closing the gap to the laser by more than half.

Daniel's grin widened. "Keep going. Can you?"

"These are the star positions of 4.8 million years ago. When the Star Beacon was abandoned."

"But that's an estimate, right? Based on meteorite pockmarks?"

"Of course. One moment." Theesah-ma voiced instructions to her hovering sphere. The stars shifted further. The orange markers representing Earth's position continued their trek to the left, eventually settling near the tip of the laser. The alignment wasn't exact, but it was close.

"Oh my," Theesah-ma said.

"Yowzers," Nala said.

Daniel felt a tingling at the back of his neck as a hunch became a certainty. "No, the Ancients didn't abandon this beacon 4.8 million years ago. I believe it was closer to six."

14 DISCOVERY

THEESAH-MA DOUBLE checked her computations. The markers did in fact represent the Sol-Earth system, though the sky in that location was dark. Nothing surprising there. A yellow dwarf a thousand light years away would be as invisible as a candle on a distant mountaintop.

"Quite startling," Theesah-ma said. "You must understand. For us, Earth is new. Our scientists had no reason to suspect the Star Beacon ever pointed to it."

"And the time estimate was off by more than a million years," Nala added. "Your scientists were searching along the wrong alignment."

Daniel nodded. "Agreed. It would be hard for anyone to find a minor star like Sol with a search direction off even by a few degrees. Frankly, I'm impressed that the Ancients found it at all, but it's clear they did. This alignment can't be a coincidence. Six million years ago, the beacon pointed to Earth."

Theesah-ma stared toward the pulsating markers almost precisely aligned at the tip of the Star Beacon's laser. Her voice became breathy, almost giddy. "Yes, I agree. Knowing a civilization is there, the alignment is certain. Lovely, Daniel... your insight..."

Nala hugged Daniel. "When this guy gets going, watch out."

"A hunch," Daniel said. "Once I saw that we were in Orion's belt, it became more than a hunch."

"Astonishing. The Ancients found you so long ago. But what happened next? They disappeared. Did they journey to your planet?"

"Now you're talking," Nala said. "These guys peered into their giganto-scope, liked what they saw, climbed into their starship, and zipped off to Earth."

Daniel shrugged. "A possible explanation, but it is a long trip. With Mintaka still in front of us, we've got to be at least a thousand light years away. Even with a high-speed starship, that's a five or ten-thousand-year journey."

Nala waved a hand. "No problem. Pop into cryogenic freeze mode, wake up on Earth. Piece of cake."

Daniel tipped his head. "Okay, maybe. Let's say their scope discovered the plentiful oxygen in our atmosphere – always a good indicator of life. And maybe they built a starship and made it all the way to Earth. But six million years ago was the late Miocene epoch. Primates dominated. Lemurs, simians. Roughly the time our ancestors split away from chimpanzees to produce the first hominins. Species like graecopithecus and orrorin tugenensis. Pretty smart, but they had no language. They weren't even toolmakers. I'm afraid the Ancients would have been sorely disappointed."

Theesah-ma cooed in a deeply satisfying bass. "I see another option." Her cephalopod head twisted to Daniel and then to Nala. If alien eyes could twinkle, hers were doing just that. "What if these ignorant beasts are not your ancestors after all. What if *you* are the Ancients?"

"Ooh," Nala said. "That would be cool."

"Fun, but not – ", Daniel started but Nala interrupted.

"Oh, come on, Daniel, play the game. My turn. What if they came to Earth to capture hominids for their interplanetary zoo?"

Daniel smiled, game on. "Fine, they're zookeepers. So, where's their zoo? I'd pay good money to see a living graecopithecus."

Nala shrugged, then waved her hands as another idea occurred. "Okay, okay." She cleared her throat. "They arrive on Earth, get bored trying to communicate with lemurs and grapo-pithy-whatever, so...

they install a homing beacon buried somewhere in the Sahara, just waiting for humans to evolve and uncover it!"

Daniel pointed a finger. "Summer blockbuster, for sure, but I think I've seen that movie."

Nala poked him in the ribs. "Starring some hunky guy as the brilliant but moody scientist."

He poked her back. "And his curvaceous love interest who inexplicably wears lace lingerie under her lab coat."

Nala waggled her eyebrows and pushed up her breasts in mock seduction.

Quietly perplexed, Theesah-ma's eyes moved between Daniel and Nala. "I have no idea what you two are talking about."

"Sorry," Daniel said. "Just something we do. Brainstorming. Throwing out options."

Nala laughed. "We come up with pretty good ideas, but sometimes we veer off track." She nudged Theesah-ma. "Hey, you started it."

"I did?"

"You did." Daniel explained. "The Ancients-are-you thing. Human evolutionary history is well established. We can link our DNA to precursor species who lived a billion years ago. So no, we're not the Ancients. We're Earthlings through and through."

"Good to hear," Theesah-ma said. "Sometimes Litian-nolo imaginations can also veer..."

"Off track," Nala finished. She hugged Theesah-ma. "It's okay. There are no wrong answers when brainstorming."

"I like this method. Brainstorming. Very resourceful. It seems... very human." Theesah-ma reached a hand to both Daniel and Nala. "Together we have discovered a connection between the Ancients and humans. Previously unknown. Quite remarkable."

Daniel nodded. "We might want to return to Jheean and let people know, especially the Colonists. Ajadu told me that he didn't know where the Ancients went, but that I did. At the time I thought he was crazy. Now…" Daniel's voice lifted up at the end. He smiled.

Now that Daniel had seen the Star Beacon, it wasn't surprising that Ajadu had made the connection to Daniel's fever dream. But his declaration that Daniel had knowledge of the Ancients was nothing more than a projection fallacy – the presumption that recent events were the answer to an age-old question. Sure, Ajadu had turned out to be partly right – they had just made a reasonable guess where the Ancients went – but that was only coincidence.

Wasn't it?

"I admit the Colonist stories could be more than myth," Theesah-ma said. "They speak of the divide. Of a grand voyage. The beacon's alignment with Earth is a compelling discovery. Yet there is more of their myth to decipher. The Colonist name, for example. It has meaning still not fully explained by our discovery today."

Theesah-ma swept a long arm across the nearly infinite beacon stretching before them. "We left to stay behind, they say. Still a puzzle."

Daniel froze. Words directly from his vision, repeated exactly as he'd remembered. *We left to stay behind, they say. Still a puzzle.* More proof that he'd witnessed this moment and yet had done nothing to make it happen. It had simply occurred as if it had always been there.

"Future memory," Daniel mumbled under his breath.

Nala noticed. "What?"

Daniel took a deep breath. "It's uh… the vision. Theesah-ma just said what I had remembered. We left to stay behind. Still a puzzle. Those exact words. A few minutes ago, she said, it draws the eye. I

132

remember her saying that too. It's all playing out right now, a future memory."

"Whoa." Nala grabbed both of his hands.

Theesah-ma said, "You seem certain. And I believe you. Lovely Daniel, lovely Nala… we have arrived at the inflection point."

Nala looked around but there weren't any physical indicators of the prophesied event. "So now what?"

"Impossible to predict. But our next actions could change the future."

"But that's always the case," Nala countered. "Even if Daniel forecasted this moment, cause still produces effect. It always has. Why would this moment be any different?"

Nala had a good point. Ever since Daniel had returned from his jump to the future, he'd grappled with the strange notion that every action he took, every word he uttered in his daily life produced a downstream effect with unknown consequences. Carried to the extreme, it could make you crazy. Did stopping at that yellow light instead of driving through the intersection avoid some fender bender further down the street? Or create a new danger that otherwise wouldn't have occurred?

Theesah-ma responded. "Not every moment is influential. A story is wrapped in description, but we recognize the climax when it comes. In their way, Litian-nolo time mentors are storytellers. They search for inflection points. Key events that reshape the story."

"And this is one?" Nala asked.

"This is one," Theesah-ma confirmed. "Your Daniel's future memory confirms it."

"So, what do we do?" Daniel asked. "What would your time mentors do?"

"They would already have a plan. Do you?"

"A plan? No. But if this inflection point is related to where the Ancients went, I do have some ideas forming – beyond our little brainstorming session."

Nala hugged him. "This guy. There's your inflection point, TM. Whatever is brewing in his head. I've seen him do it. He comes up with things."

Theesah-ma glanced up to the Star Beacon's laser, then back to Daniel. "Yes, the Star Beacon is the key. Were you aware that the Council of Equivalence meets at this moment? They will decide if humans are admitted to Sagittarius Novus."

"Yeah, we heard," Daniel said. "Our representative, Secretary Jensen, didn't seem to think things were going very well. You think the attacks against me are part of it?"

"Indirectly, yes. They attack whatever you will do next. What is *in your head*, as your lovely Nala says. You have opponents, Chorl the Torak, and…" She wrapped her jointed arms around both humans in a group hug. "Hataki-ka too, I am afraid."

"The Litian-nolo time mentor?" Nala asked. "The guy who told you Daniel was… what did you call it?"

"An instigator. Yes, Hataki-ka warned me. Encouraged me to stop Daniel. An inflection point is a delicate balance. Time mentors are wise, but…"

"But now you've seen what the inflection point is all about," Daniel said. "The Star Beacon is proof there is a connection between Ancients and humans even if we're still guessing how things played out millions of years ago. And if humans are the key to this mystery, it's a discovery that could affect the council's decision on whether we become members."

"Exactly," Theesah-ma said. "This is the delicate balance of the inflection point. The council's vote could go either way."

Nala said, "And if humans are rejected, then we might end up like the Sandzvallons – shunned. Pushed off into our little corner of the galaxy with just enough knowledge of time manipulation to ensure we fail spectacularly."

The connection to the council vote matched the future events Daniel had glimpsed, but alien motivations weren't clear. The Torak had literally tried to kill him – twice. "Why do Chorl and Hataki-ka want us to fail?"

"Chorl is nothing," Theesah-ma said. "Toraks are time apprentices. Unskilled, but eager. But Chorl will follow as Hataki-ka leads. I have underestimated Hataki-ka's contempt. He speaks of human ignorance. Of human weapons. Of warfare. We all do. Litian-nolos see the weaknesses of your race. But there is more that Hataki-ka and others do not appreciate."

Nala looked up to the giant. "And now that you know us, you recognize our better side?"

Theesah-ma's eyes glistened. "I do. I was foolish not to grasp Hataki-ka's plan. Like you, Daniel, Hataki-ka has a future memory of this moment. He has surely noticed the human connection to the Ancients."

Daniel felt the truth in Theesah-ma's statements. "He tried to manipulate events, using you and Chorl to stop us."

The edges of her flat head wobbled in a wave that went from bottom to top, almost the opposite of the curl that represented a smile. "I am so sorry, lovely Daniel."

"Not your fault," Daniel said. "At least we know where we stand. And we're glad to have you on our side." He ran a hand across the giant's bony shoulder, oddly soft even though the skin provided little padding. "Let's get back to Jheean. Tell Zin. Tell Secretary Jensen."

"Yes, but safely," Theesah-ma advised. "Chorl may still be searching for you. He has already shown he can control s-bots. I will contact your Zin, but we will need to hide while waiting. And I have just the place. Come!"

Theesah-ma led back through the invisible torus, around the Star Beacon and the teardrop-shaped star that fed it. Daniel glanced back at the beacon's laser, still pointing to the markers Theesah-ma had placed in the sky.

The mystery of the Ancients had only been partially solved. Questions still swirled in Daniel's head. Why was Earth so special? What had they noticed in the images provided by their impressive telescope? And why abandon such a magnificent instrument to journey so far away? Theesah-ma might call it a human connection, but whatever drove the Ancients had nothing to do with humans, who wouldn't evolve for millions of years.

There was still more to uncover, and the answers felt tantalizingly close.

Hurrying through the torus, they arrived back at the portal. Theesah-ma stopped. She held out a suckered hand. "Your security tokens. One step into Jheean, and they will know. But I have a solution."

Daniel pulled the thin wafer from his pocket and gave it to Theesah-ma. Nala did the same.

"Cover your eyes. It may become hot for a moment." Theesah-ma pressed a control on the portal's edge. A green glow lit around them, revealing the curving surface of the physical tube they'd been inside all along. Daniel covered his eyes as instructed but peeked between fingers.

Theesah-ma retrieved a small metal box from the pocket in her dress and slid its cover open. She retrieved a round ball of white wax and pressed it against the green glow of the torus's tube. It stuck easily. She secured both wafers to the waxy blob, then stood back.

With a verbal command to her floating sphere, the wax ignited in a bright flash and a loud pop. The mini explosion blew a hole about the size of a dinner plate in the tube's wall. Air rushed out. Intense heat from the nearby star poured in. For a brief moment, it felt like standing next to a pottery kiln in a hurricane.

Just as quickly, the shattered tube magically repaired itself. The hole sealed and the airflow stopped as if someone had slammed a hatch shut. Outside, burning wreckage of broken glass, exploding wax, and two security tokens careened toward the star.

Nala was wide-eyed. "Damn girl, you said you were a scientist, but you never mentioned you were also a demolition expert."

Daniel took a deep breath. "You knew the tube would fix itself?"

Theesah-ma shrugged her bony shoulders. "Best to dispose of the tokens where no one will notice."

The melted glob plunged onward to its final demise on the star's surface. Theesah-ma pointed to the mirrored surface of the portal. "You are safe from detection now. Shall we?"

15 RHUBARB

THEESAH-MA'S JHEEAN apartment turned out to be more than a temporary refuge from spitting Toraks and unruly Litian-nolo time mentors. With a ceiling that soared to cathedral heights and a window overlooking a lush garden, it was a magnificent place to spend their time while waiting for Zin to join.

Nala was already pressed up against the floor-to-ceiling glass. "Rhubarb trees?"

Just outside, reddish-purple stalks grew as tall as any tree on Earth. Each trunk had rhubarb coloring and a celery cross section with one side concave and the other convex. Purple foliage capped the top of the plants as they reached high overhead to a glass dome. A cliff of broken boulders complemented the exotic terrarium and a stream cascaded down the rocks into a pool below. Small puffs of fur floated in the water, either decorations or sedate aquatic animals. Disney couldn't have done a better job of creating an outdoor scene, indoors.

"Nice place you have here, TM," Nala said sniffing the air. Daniel had noticed it too, a distinct smell of sulfur. Not overbearing. More like vacationing at a thermal hot spring.

"Used only when I am at Jheean." Theesah-ma had stretched to her full height with the ceiling still well above her head. A loft tucked into one side of the room with a ladder inset on the wall. Rungs were spaced at intervals taller than a human. This apartment was clearly designed for giants.

She removed the breathing apparatus from her face, revealing a skin flap that opened and closed in rhythmic breathing. "If the hydrogen sulfide bothers you, I can cleanse the air."

"Reminds me of Yellowstone," Nala said taking a deep breath. "I like it."

Theesah-ma showed Daniel to a tall, narrow closet explaining that cleansing the air wasn't the only technology in her apartment. The molecular disassociation chamber, as she called it, was ideally suited for people who had recently returned from the desert. He did smell a bit and the lower portion of his pants were mottled with dried salt. Theesah-ma was gracious but insistent.

The procedure didn't even require removing his clothes. Once the door closed, swirling mist poured from tiny slits all around. With an ultrasonic vibration that made his teeth chatter, and a touch of fragrance smelling vaguely of lime, he was soon fresh as a daisy – skin and clothes.

Stepping out, Daniel said, "Thanks for the shower. I guess I needed it."

"You did," Nala whispered, kissing him. "No more desert survival tests. I'm not letting you out of my sight." Once her fury had been fueled by injustice, Nala made a fierce partner. Chorl wouldn't stand a chance against her. Even attacking s-bots would be dispatched with ease.

Zin would arrive soon, increasing confidence that physical conflicts were behind them. Two determined humans along with their trusty android guide, backed up by a Colonist bartender and a Litian-nolo scientist made for an unusual collaboration, but potentially effective in their diversity. With a little luck, they even had a chance to help poor Secretary Jensen, who at this moment was defending humanity in a political battle within the council chambers.

Theesah-ma took a seat on a padded bench at the base of a curving lavender wall, then repositioned her floating spherical device. She spoke in her native language – fluid and songlike, with lilting tones that uplifted the end of each phrase. Some words sounded vaguely Japanese – *miezo, ushimah*, and *dojoko*. It seemed a language that humans might learn to speak given more time among the Litian-nolos.

"I have asked for refreshments from the kitchen. Join me and we will speak more of the Star Beacon while we await your Zin."

Daniel and Nala took seats on either side of the giant, Nala requiring a boost to reach the chest-high cushion. Their feet dangled like kids in an adult chair.

Moments later, a floating metal cylinder – a skinnier version of a scuba diver's air tank – zipped from behind a corner. It carried three trays, each crowded with a variety of small pots. The flying cylinder distributed one tray to each person then zipped away. The trays floated without support – graviton manipulation on display once more.

Nala opened one of the steaming pots, sniffed, then poured the black liquid into a narrow silver cup. "Coffee." She stretched out the word like a junkie demanding her fix.

"*Ichi mak*. Similar to your coffee, I hope," Theesah-ma said, pouring her own. She folded articulated legs under her dress and leaned to the back of the couch.

Nala sipped. Her satisfied expression made it clear the Litian-nolo version was as good as any on Earth. The small pots all held something different, and while Daniel wasn't excited to try the wiggling pink prongs, the crackers looked good. For her part, Nala sampled them all, her expression varying from doubt to delight as she tasted each one.

The room was comfortable, Zin had been notified of their location, and best of all, they were past the mysterious inflection point. "I've been thinking about the beacon on our way back to Jheean."

"Stand back," Nala said. "That brain of his is churning."

She knew him well. New thoughts had kicked off when Theesah-ma had asked if he had a plan for the inflection point, and Nala had poured on the encouragement. Funny thing about encouragement, it works.

Daniel pointed out Theesah-ma's apartment window to the forest of oversized rhubarbs. "Typical of your planet?"

One of Theesah-ma's eyes glanced independently to the red-purple plants and back to Daniel. "We have a great variety of life on our planet. These are only a few."

"How many of your plants are green?"

"Ah, green plants. So exotic. I have seen photographs of Earth. Your planet is lovely."

Ajadu had said much the same thing – green plants were thought of as exotic. It confirmed Daniel's hunch, but he'd need more than just their opinions.

Daniel laid out the basics of a still-forming hypothesis. "On Earth, two complex organic molecules evolved, retinal and chlorophyll. Both use sunlight to fulfill a plant's energy needs, but chlorophyll takes the process one step further by fixing carbon from the air to build plant structure. Retinal plants rely on a nucleotide for creating their structures – a bit less efficient. Chemically, the two molecules are similar. But at its core, chlorophyll contains a ringlike structure called a porphyrin with a magnesium atom at the center. That single difference is everything when it comes to color. Retinal absorbs green, leaving blue and red reflected – we see that as purple. Chlorophyll is just the opposite, absorbing blue and red, but leaving green reflected."

"How well you explain it, lovely Daniel."

"He's got the explanation stuff down," Nala agreed. "This guy has a stockpile of scientific facts for every occasion. Okay, scientist, where are you going with this colorful botany?"

Daniel's eyes wandered up the stalks of rhubarb outside the window. "In the Bektash desert there are purple topped mountains and purple palms by the sea. At first, I figured Bektash was the oddity but the more I learn, it seems retinal is dominant not just here but on many planets.

"I can query for you." Theesah-ma gave a voice command and her ever-present floating sphere popped up a blue screen in the air. After a few more commands, it displayed a page of alien text along with photographs of green plants. "Earth is not the only world with green plants. We have discovered fourteen others."

"Data. I do love data. That gives us a numerator, now we just need a denominator. How many planets are there with *any* kind of life? Plants, animals. Even bacteria."

"Everyone asks this question. The answer requires no search. One of our universities posts a tally they call the Life Count. It is updated as new life is discovered anywhere in the galaxy. I believe there are now more than three thousand planets."

"And there you have it," Daniel said. "Fifteen out of three thousand. Earth is a one-half of one-percent aberration. As you say, green plants are exotic. Your numbers just proved it."

Theesah-ma set her silver cup down on the floating tray. "How interesting."

Nala mimicked Theesah-ma's soothing voice. "Yes, how very interesting indeed." She set her alien coffee cup down too. "I see where you're going with this – I think."

Their attention captured, Daniel gathered in his mind the details to complete his hypothesis. They came easily. Daniel had always been a storyteller, a quality he shared with Ajadu, though Daniel's stories emerged from science.

"Journey back in time with me. Six million years ago. The Ancients have pointed their mega-telescope at promising targets across the sky. Eventually they lock onto Earth. Their scope has enough resolution to examine its surface and its atmosphere. What do they find? No evidence of civilization or technology. No CO_2 buildup. No unnatural molecules in the atmosphere that might indicate a civilization. Maybe they even send a laser message with their powerful beacon, but they get no reply."

"Low brain power residents," Nala said.

"Right. Graecopithecus is just figuring out how to chisel a sharp edge onto a piece of flint. Best he can do."

"She."

"She."

Nala tilted her head, thinking. "So… if the Ancients were only searching for civilizations, they'd note this planet in their logbooks then point their mega-scope somewhere else. But that's not what happened." The light had already switched on for Nala.

Daniel continued. "Right. The Star Beacon never moved again. Something about Earth drew their attention. Convinced them a trip, even a lengthy trip, was worth their time. They discovered chlorophyll, a molecule they hadn't seen before. Its spectral signature looked like retinal, but with the addition of magnesium – tantalizingly different, perhaps even unnatural. After all, the Ancients were genetic engineers. They were used to inserting new bits into their own DNA. They even created a religion around it.

"Maybe they decided that chlorophyll was a version of retinal that had been intentionally modified. Maybe they saw this new molecule as evidence of another race of genetic engineers roaming the galaxy. From their perspective, Earth was a planet worth exploring."

Nala agreed. "It's a solid motive. Curiosity took over and they sent ships."

"But not just any ships. What if the Colonist story of the Great Divide is true? Their population split, with a significant portion beginning a long journey of discovery."

"So, we're talking big ships."

"Star cruisers engineered to support a population willing to cross the galaxy in search of splendid curiosities. Ten thousand years enroute, maybe longer. Without portals, their answer to the vast distances between stars was to engineer their lifetimes. If you live to a hundred-thousand years, even a trip to Earth is within reach."

Theesah-ma watched, providing no contribution to the analysis but paying full attention. Her head moved back and forth between Daniel and Nala on either side.

"Okay," Nala said, "I buy that as a working theory, but where's the evidence? If they came to Earth six million years ago, there's probably no trace of their visit."

"No buried monoliths in the Sahara?" Daniel smiled.

"Nope. They just park in orbit, collect a few plants, ignore the monkeys swinging from the trees, and move on."

"Well, our ancestors at the time were a little better than monkeys. And they weren't swinging from the trees."

"But they couldn't communicate. Back then, the best we could offer was the grapo-pithy-guy, or... what did you call it?"

"Orrorin tugenensis. Dwellers of the African savanna, but yeah, probably not a very conversant fellow. Bipedal, though."

"But no radio, no lasers, no language. I agree, chlorophyll may have caught their attention, but I wonder..." As she worked out her question, the words came slowly. "Once they collected our nice green plants, then what? Wouldn't they go home? And if they did, why is the Star Beacon still pointing to Earth? Well... where Earth was located six million years ago."

It was a ragged edge to his still-forming theory. Nala was good at finding holes. Daniel shrugged, thinking through options. "The beacon served as a breadcrumb trail?"

"A way to find their way back?"

"Right."

Nala scrunched up her nose and shook her head with conviction. "No way. An interstellar starship captain that needs a laser pointer to find her way home is a pretty lousy celestial navigator."

"Okay then... maybe the beam powered a light sail."

Nala nodded. "Better. Their whopper laser does have the energy of a star behind it."

"You are doing it again, aren't you?" Theesah-ma asked. She'd been watching the back and forth like a tennis match.

Daniel looked up at Theesah-ma. "What, brainstorming? Just something we do."

"All the time," Nala added.

Theesah-ma's eyes still darted between them. "Such a clever process. As a scientist, I am fascinated. As a friend, watching your interaction is a pleasure. Can I call you friends?"

Nala wrapped a hand around the suckered tip of Theesah-ma's arm. "Of course. In our culture, people can be new friends or old friends. Doesn't matter."

She cooed. "I enjoy watching the way humans think. The interplay between you. The questions you ask yourselves. Your curiosity. For you, the Colonists' story is of great interest."

"Very much," Daniel said. "If we believe Colonist folklore, the lifespan of the Ancients could reach a hundred thousand years. What do you do with that kind of time? What journeys might you be willing to take?" Daniel paced, staring at the floor. He stopped. "Hmm."

Nala set her cup down hard, spilling a few drops from the rather unstable narrow cup. Humans probably had something to contribute when it came to tableware. "What?"

"Just a thought."

"Spill it. Well, don't spill it. You know what I mean."

"Living for a hundred thousand years would certainly give you a different perspective." He tapped his upper lip. "A ten-thousand-year trip? Easy. But what if it was longer?"

More puzzle pieces floated through his mind. Dots connected, the final piece coming from left field. Daniel looked up at his companions. "What if they never built any starships? What if they decided on a slow cruise instead? Taking... millions of years."

Nala clarified. "You're saying the Ancients took millions of years to get to Earth?"

"Yeah, I am, but more than that. Who says their journey is finished?"

16 COUNCIL

DANIEL WAS SURE he had the answers. Ninety-five percent sure, and that last five percent wouldn't be hard to fill in. It was a satisfying feeling, like holding a jigsaw puzzle piece between your fingers, confident that it will fit perfectly into the irregular hole that has frustrated everyone else for hours.

They'd done the calculations. Checked and double-checked the results. Even pulled out an electronic protractor from Theesah-ma's handy hovering sphere to check the angles.

He'd figured out not only *where* the Ancients had gone – Earth, unquestionably – but *how* their epic journey had played out. Better still, he had a hunch their journey was still in progress, assuming this long-lived race hadn't died out as the millennia passed. Evidence – though unconfirmed – lined up seamlessly in his mind.

Daniel was halfway through an explanation when Zin arrived at Theesah-ma's apartment. After a quick summary, Zin agreed that Daniel's newest theory of the Ancients had legs. "You must present your ideas to the council, Dr. Rice. Many representatives will be interested, even captivated. But we must hurry. Secretary Jensen is in an awful position."

The Council of Equivalence had apparently erupted into a chaos of competing voices – all debating whether humans should be admitted or turned away from Sagittarius Novus. A theory that connected the highly revered Ancients to the planet Earth could change the debate, or at least act as a diversion to calm the chaos.

All because of a visit to the Star Beacon.

It had been an inflection point, just as Theesah-ma had said, but its possibilities for good or bad were still playing out. Humanity's chances for galactic membership balanced on a razor's edge but

Daniel's newest idea felt like an ace up the sleeve. Now he just needed a seat at the table – and that would be up to Zin.

They split up, with Theesah-ma heading to a Litian-nolo office where backdoor channels might provide leverage, and Daniel and Nala following Zin. A minute later, they were speeding down the main avenue of Jheean on light ovals.

Zin slowed and hopped off in front of the inner hexagon's jet-black wall. Built from refrigerator sized blocks, the wall stretched left and right without breaks. On the other side was the heart of Jheean where diplomats from all twenty-three species of Sagittarius Novus mixed.

Zin strode with purpose toward a hemisphere at the wall's base where a contingent of s-bots congregated. He flashed his blue security token then squealed high-pitched words in s-bot speech. It seemed to do the trick because Daniel and Nala were waved through like VIPs entering an exclusive club.

"Well, that was easy," Daniel whispered to Nala.

Zin, whose hearing was said to be better than a big-eared bat, whispered back, "Theesah-ma greased the steps."

"Greased the skids." Zin was courageous in his regular attempts at human idioms but usually missed by a sliver.

"Skids. Yes. Theesah-ma's doing."

Always good to have friends.

It turned out to be the first of several security stations. Next was a light beam that scanned them head to foot then sprayed a pungent mist. A chemical tracer, Zin explained, that worked with an atmospheric cleansing system to expunge stray skin cells. Apparently, some members of Sagittarius Novus required serious protection from the flakier species, such as humans.

They followed Zin down a dark hallway to a third station where a tiny hummingbird bot buzzed around their heads. It pinched a blue plastic fob on one ear lobe – not painful, but slightly annoying.

Nala flicked a finger across the dangling plastic. "Humiliation complete. I feel like a dairy cow."

"My apologies, Dr. Pasquier. Required for visitors." Zin was apparently exempt; he didn't have ears anyway.

"It'll be worth it," Daniel said. He was anxious to view the inner workings of this collection of civilizations – and participate if allowed. Secretary Jensen had been fighting alone for too long.

The narrow hallway opened dramatically to a vast space bigger than any domed stadium. They stood on a platform within another of Jheean's ubiquitous glass enclosures. Overhead, dozens of tubes colored gray, green, and orange crisscrossed in a virtual spaghetti bowl of passageways going in every direction. The London Underground map had nothing on this mashup of colored tubes.

At the platform's edge, three openings presented options for entering the melee. Zin chose the middle tube. Daniel and Nala followed, happy to find it big enough to stand fully upright. The tube bent upward, an ascent that wasn't difficult given a rough floor that provided traction. Another tube crossed overhead filled with cloudy water. In it, a squid-like creature dressed in stiff armor swam toward some unknown destination.

A narrow tube crossed beneath their feet. Dark smoke billowed down its length making it difficult to see what might be inside. Several more tubes circled at other levels, some in parallel to their own.

"Gerbil heaven," Nala laughed, one step ahead of Daniel. "Is the spinning exercise wheel next?"

Another tube was filled with mustard colored gas. Slender green stalks rising from white bulbs marched down its passageway. At their base, dozens of rapidly undulating white feet completed the appearance of freshly picked scallions. Lifeforms in the oxygen petal they'd left behind seemed ordinary by comparison.

"Where is everyone going?" Nala asked.

Zin called back. "Despite the complexity, there are only three destinations. In our case, the Council of Equivalence."

The maze of passageways was difficult to sort, but as their tube bent gently left, a colossal silver orb came into view. It looked like an oversized tea pot inexplicably plugged into a gerbil maze.

Daniel had imagined a courthouse fronted by statues and white columns. Inside, alien judges would sit in a row behind an immense judicial bench. Wearing robes. And possibly white wigs.

"Reality surprises," Daniel said to himself.

"What?" Nala asked.

"Nothing. Just hoping Secretary Jensen is managing, that's all. After seeing Jheean's inner sanctum, it would be a crying shame to be excluded just because we're warlike."

"Which we're not."

"Well..." Most science fiction stories depicted aliens as vicious warriors bent on destroying every outpost of civilization for no reason other than blood lust or domination. A classic case of projection. "Maybe our better nature will show through this time."

Like punching a Torak? Self-defense, he convinced himself, though the council might see it differently. Hopefully, fist fights with aliens were behind them now.

The tube ended at another glass-enclosed platform. Zin ushered them up a short ramp where they emerged to a classic theater balcony.

Several human-sized chairs were haphazardly positioned across a red carpeted floor. Secretary General Nikolaus Jensen sat next to a young Asian woman, looking over a chaotic scene below.

No sedate courtroom, no pompous wigged judges, the council chamber was more like a boxing arena. A jumble of balconies and bubbles were crowded with members from every species imaginable, some familiar, some unrecognizable. The collection of seating areas overlooked a central stage where electronic avatars of different species mingled like actors in a play.

Nala held a hand to her mouth. "Like being thrown into a toy box, packed with sci-fi action figures."

Secretary Jensen looked up, smiled, and waved them in. Nala and Daniel took seats next to Jensen. Zin remained standing at the balcony entrance.

"You made it!" Jensen said. "I can't tell you how reassuring it is to see more of our kind." Jensen introduced them to his aide, Kim Jiwoo. Four humans among dozens of other species.

"Tough day for you too, huh?" Daniel asked.

"I'll tell you later." Jensen reached for a hovering sphere at his shoulder. Superior alien technology had been made available to the primitive humans. There was hope for them yet. "Zin messaged me that you two were coming. And provided the gist of your... shall we call it the Theory of Dissat? Daniel, I must say, a remarkable idea."

"Will we get time to present it?"

Jensen shrugged. "Maybe. I'll try, but things are escalating rapidly." Jensen returned his attention to the boxing arena's central stage where several avatars faced off.

Daniel poked Nala and pointed to the neighboring balcony occupied by Litian-nolos. Except for their clothing, the four lanky giants occupying it looked no different than Theesah-ma. Nala caught their attention with a wave, and all four waved back.

"At least, we've got friends," she whispered. The current speaker wore a blue vest and silver pants, helpful to tell them apart. None wore a red dress, but they hadn't expected Theesah-ma to be among the delegation.

In the next balcony over, a group of tiny hedgehogs sat on booster seats, just tall enough to see over the railing. Their leader stood on a small platform at the edge of the balcony, jabbering in squeaks as its quilled, white-bellied avatar on stage spoke.

"Oh my god, they are so adorable," Nala whispered. "I had two hamsters when I was a kid, but I always wanted a hedgehog."

"Intelligent hedgehogs," Daniel reminded. "I bet one or two of them would be happy to talk physics with you."

On stage, a translucent Torak avatar faced off against a white-robed Colonist and a Litian-nolo. The hedgehog stood to one side, its quills flattened along its back like arrows ready for any battle that might erupt. The avatars looked and moved realistically around the stage but there was one significant difference. Equal heights. On stage, the tiny hedgehog was just as tall as the giant Litian-nolo.

"The Council of Equivalence," Jensen pointed out. "Litian-nolos or Chitzas, it doesn't matter. Every species takes the stage without bias."

Chitzas. Daniel recalled the name from a list of known species, but sometimes a name and photo weren't enough to conjure reality. When the Chitza in the neighboring balcony squeaked, its avatar on stage mimicked at a volume equal to the others, and English words came from a panel just in front of Jensen. Communication among multiple species had been solved, at least for this chamber.

The avatar for the centipede-like Torak seemed agitated. It waved ribbed fans in the air. Physical shushes of air were easily heard even though the Torak balcony was on the opposite side of the arena. "How dare you suggest..." came the translation.

The Colonist onstage raised a fisted bird claw. "Don't even try."

"I can see what you've been up against," Daniel whispered to Jensen. "And *we're* the warlike species?"

Jensen smiled. He'd been here on and off for weeks and had probably witnessed every possible interaction among these exotically different sentients.

Sitting at Jensen's right, his aide Jiwoo leaned across. "You should have seen the food fight last week. Took me three air showers to get all the Chitza bananas off my clothes."

Daniel raised an eyebrow. Not exactly behavior he'd expect from galactic intelligences, but weaponized food was probably better than alien energy blasters.

On stage, the Torak's avatar mimicked the physical movements of the speaker. Arm fans flared and snapped shut with the same movements Daniel had seen prior to the demise of poor Tozz. Spittle spewed from a gap in the Torak's helmet.

Are Toraks always this angry? Daniel wondered. At least one of these creatures was responsible for throwing Daniel and Tozz into the desert. But which? On Earth, accusations made against an entire race came from fools on the wrong side of history. Daniel observed with care.

The Torak speaker wasn't alone in the balcony. A second Torak stood quietly to one side. Its helmet was dented.

"That's the guy." Daniel pointed out the individual to Jensen.

"An assistant to the Torak diplomat, I believe," Jensen said. "That one has been in and out all day. It must be conferring with others outside the chamber."

"Or trying to kill humans. Me specifically." Jensen raised a brow and Daniel gave him a brief rundown of the clash at the portal, including Tozz's self-destruct command. Jensen absorbed the tale, his expression becoming stern as Daniel concluded.

Jensen kept his voice low. "We're allowed three interruptions. I've already used up two, but this may be worth the third." He conferred with Jiwoo who left the balcony along with Zin. When she returned a few minutes later she was all smiles.

"We've got them now," Jiwoo said. She accessed a popup screen from her own floating sphere and pointed Jensen to rows of data that appeared in the air.

Jensen nodded, then spoke to Daniel and Nala. "Cross your fingers. This won't be easy, but the data is in our favor."

Jensen stood up. A human avatar looking remarkably like him appeared on stage equal in height to the others. "I have news," Jensen said in a loud voice.

The argument between the Torak and the Colonist suddenly calmed. Murmurs died. Every alien light sensor in the arena turned to the human balcony.

Jensen's booming voice was enough to fill the now-quiet arena while twenty-three translations echoed from each of the balconies. "I have just received word that a security bot – under direct orders from a Torak – has been destroyed."

Daniel was a little miffed that the headline was the destruction of a security bot instead of a threat to a human life, but the uptick in murmurs around the arena seemed to confirm that Jensen had chosen the right way to frame it.

"We deny such falsehood," the Torak diplomat shushed. "Humans lie."

Jensen stood his ground. "As diplomats, you each have access to Jheean security records. Please examine the records recently uploaded by s-bot three one zero zero just before its demise."

Wow. Nice job Tozz.

Daniel choked up. A hero was a hero, regardless of its construction. Nala reached for his hand and squeezed tight. With no idea what might happen next, they watched in interest as a flurry of activity spread across the arena. Diplomats reached for their communication spheres. Hovering popups appeared everywhere, no doubt listing the same data Jiwoo had pulled up. Seconds later, murmurs began again.

The Colonist on stage spoke for them all. "This s-bot arrested a human. Twice."

"Of course, it did," the Torak said. "The bot was doing its job. Additional humans have not been authorized at Jheean, per this council's decision."

The Colonist countered, "But the records indicate direct commands issued by a Torak. Chorl, a member of the Torak delegation."

"Advice only!" the Torak countered. "S-bots are security agents under Core's command. Their mission is sacred within these walls. We all respect their autonomy."

Jensen was quick to respond. "S-bot three one zero zero self-destructed rather than carry out your so-called *advice*." His emphasis was strong, creating quite a stir across the audience.

"Self-destruction. Sssh. Another human lie. At this moment, the s-bot's status is active. See for yourself!"

Daniel whispered to Jensen. "Active? That's not possible. I watched Tozz blow its head off."

Jiwoo grimaced as she examined another screen. "The Torak is right. I see the self-destruct sequence faithfully recorded but for some reason the s-bot is still listed as active. Not sure what's going on there."

Jensen looked frustrated. Daniel and Nala exchanged a worried glance.

The Torak shouted. "As I said, humans cannot be trusted. Toraks have no control over s-bots. This bot was doing its duty and still is."

On stage, angry avatars stood within inches of each other, looking like they might come to blows any minute. Shouts came from around the room with additional avatars winking into and out of existence on the stage. Jensen joined the fray, but the Torak seemed to be gaining the upper hand, yelling that a vote was required.

In the neighboring balcony the Litian-nolo with the blue vest stood up. Its full height dominated the arena even if its avatar on stage did not. "Keisi mao." Its native words were spoken in a calm, but serious voice. The translation came quickly. "I have news."

They were the same words Jensen had used to interrupt, and they performed the same magic. The argument on stage died down. Attention turned to the Litian-nolo who stretched to its full height in the neighboring balcony.

"We can confirm the s-bot was destroyed. And we have learned that a Litian-nolo was involved."

17 JOURNEY

THE COUNCIL ARENA erupted in shouts and motion across every balcony overlooking the stage. Arms and tentacles waved. Hives buzzed. Fur ruffled. News that a Litian-nolo time mentor was involved in the subversion and destruction of a member of the Jheean security force clearly carried weight, especially since a Litian-nolo diplomat had made the accusation.

In the neighboring balcony, the blue-vested giant dipped its cephalopod head toward Daniel, Nala, and Secretary Jensen. Its voice was as smooth as Theesah-ma's but with hints of baritone in certain lilts. "I am Seishu-kai-do."

Nala waved at the lanky giant, then whispered to her fellow humans, "He's their big cheese. Theesah-ma told me about him."

Secretary Jensen nodded. "And Litian-nolos are well regarded among council diplomats. This should be good."

Seishu-kai-do spoke to a hushed crowd. "Our investigation concluded minutes ago. One of our time mentors, Hataki-ka, has admitted collusion with the Toraks."

There were gasps around the arena.

"My girlfriend did that," Nala said, smiling. "Nice job, TM."

On cue, another giant entered the Litian-nolo balcony. She wore a red dress, and when Nala swiveled to look, Theesah-ma gave a small wave.

Seishu-kai-do continued. "As you know, Litian-nolo time mentors manipulate inflection points, a powerful technology. We take great care to isolate timeline impacts exclusively to our planet and our species, a strict guideline backed by Core. However, in a recent case, we have faltered. An egregious error, and I humbly apologize to every member."

Seishu-kai-do raised one bony limb. "But there is good news. Working with the humans, one of our scientists has successfully deflected damage from the manipulated inflection point. We believe Theesah-ma, in coordination with Core, has contained the downstream temporal impacts."

Daniel and Nala bumped fists. Theesah-ma gently bowed her head.

"With Core's assistance, we will now conduct a full sweep of neighboring inflection points to be sure there are no residual effects. Punishment will be assessed for our time mentor, but only this council can address the Torak collusion. I request an official inquiry."

The Torak avatar had already fled the stage. Several Toraks huddled in their balcony like corrupt politicians caught with their hands in the till.

A new avatar appeared on stage, squid-like, with multiple tentacles wriggling from beneath a plate of armor – one of the species they'd passed in the maze of tubes. Its voice quavered like it was speaking through bubbles in water. "As conflict adjudicators for the council, a Sundasti inquisition team will be assembled to examine the Litian-nolo evidence. We will, of course, seek responses from both Toraks and Litian-nolos. However, bylaws do not cover non-members. Humans cannot be represented in this inquiry."

Voices sounded around the arena. Jensen was just about to stand up when Seishu-kai-do spoke. "We thank the Sundasti adjudicators and will cooperate fully. As for the humans, may I suggest another approach?" Seishu-kai-do turned toward Jensen. "I am told that humans have completed a separate investigation but one derived from the inflection point. It involves the Star Beacon, of interest to every species of Sagittarius Novus and may have bearing on the Sundasti inquiry. Since humans cannot be represented in the inquiry, I ask that we yield time to them now. Their discovery is quite remarkable."

Tentacles on the Sundasti avatar twitched uncontrollably. "The Star Beacon? How curious. Yes, of course. I yield to the humans."

Every face, every eye, every snout, and wiggling appendage turned toward the human balcony. A hush fell over the crowd. Jensen spoke quietly to Daniel. "This is all yours. You okay with that?"

Daniel gave him a thumbs up and stood. An avatar of Daniel appeared on stage, no configuration required.

He cleared his throat, which echoed through the translating devices at each balcony. "Thank you. We're honored to be here. My name is Daniel Rice, I'm a scientist. My wife and colleague, Nala Pasquier, and I represented humanity when we made first contact with Core three years ago."

The stillness in the room was eerie. Daniel wondered if Jensen had also received a stony reception when he'd first spoken.

"Earlier today, I was outside in the desert heat – not by choice. It seems someone didn't want me here. They threw s-bot Three One Zero Zero outside too, probably to eliminate evidence, but I'll leave that investigation to you. While I wandered the desert, I met a Colonist named Ajadu who told me the remarkable story of the Ancients."

The Colonist avatar still on stage nodded with recognition of Ajadu's name.

Daniel continued, summarizing what he'd learned about Colonist lifetimes, the mythology of their ancestors, and of the Great Divide. He kept his words to a minimum since by Theesah-ma's account, the Colonist story was common knowledge, even if some species didn't believe it.

"When Ajadu and I returned to the Jheean citadel, we were confronted by a Torak, and I was arrested. I watched that s-bot self-destruct." There were more murmurs around the arena, confirming that messing with an s-bot was a shocking act of subversion. He didn't bother explaining that his life had also been in danger.

Daniel pointed to Theesah-ma, now folded to half size at the back of the Litian-nolo balcony. "Do you want to explain how we made the discovery?"

"I can do better," Theesah-ma said in English. "I can show them." She stretched to full height and stepped to the front of the balcony. An avatar in a slim red dress appeared on stage, the same height as Daniel's.

With a touch of her floating sphere, a three-dimensional rotating galaxy appeared above the stage. Millions of tiny points of light mixed with clouds of darker dust and glowing gas to nearly fill the arena – a three-dimensional graphic worthy of a special effects award. With a wave from her suckered hand, the galactic map zoomed in to a dull red star near the middle of one spiral arm. A filament of fire pulled away from the star, sucked into a parabolic mirror. The Star Beacon's red laser flashed across a field of stars, finally ending at a yellow sun where a blue and white planet orbited.

Theesah-ma cooed in her native language, the translation echoing around the chamber. "For centuries, we all thought the Star Beacon pointed to nothing. New data tells a different story. We now believe our estimate for the date of its abandonment was wrong. Almost four hundred thousand seasons, or six million years ago, this ancient beacon pointed to the human planet, Earth."

The arena buzzed with excitement confirming their interest in the ancient story and validating that any explanation from a Litian-nolo scientist was well respected.

"We knew our discovery was profound, but it created more questions than it answered. Why should the beacon point to Earth? We had ideas, but no evidence. In this, the humans have been most helpful." Theesah-ma looked to Daniel and Nala, her flat head curling around the edges in an expression they'd come to know as a smile. "Please, listen as Daniel explains. You will see as I have – he is quite good at this."

Her encouragement was all Daniel needed. The components of his theory were laid out in his mind, and the splendid graphic hovering over the arena was a bonus he wasn't expecting.

"Have you seen photographs of Earth?" A rhetorical question, he wasn't really expecting a show of hands. "If so, you may have noticed we have green plants – a rarity, as I've only recently learned. Scan two hundred planets with life, and odds are you'll find only one that has the chlorophyll chemistry that produces this color."

Above the rotating galaxy, a new three-dimensional image popped up – a complexity of colored balls arranged in a tadpole shape. Daniel immediately noticed the familiar central circle of its structure: four nitrogen atoms surrounding a magnesium atom. Theesah-ma had managed to locate and project a model of the chlorophyll molecule. Bravo.

Daniel pointed. "Six million years ago, this unusual molecule – found only on Earth and a few other places – caught the attention of the Ancients. Sufficiently, I believe, to motivate some of them to set sail for my home planet in an event the Colonists call the Great Divide."

There were murmurs around the arena. Daniel had expected as much, but he hadn't even begun to detail the crux of his idea, the Theory of Dissat as Secretary Jensen had decided it should be called.

In the Colonist balcony, a new figure arrived and lowered the hood of his robe. Like Daniel and Nala, a blue visitor tag dangled like an earring from the side of his beaked head.

Daniel waved an arm toward Ajadu. "Our Colonist friends have explained to me the Ancients' reverence for genetic manipulation, their religion and their god, the Designer. This history may be related."

Daniel pointed to the floating model of chlorophyll. Theesah-ma's graphic aids were coming in handy.

"Long ago, as the Ancients studied Earth through their powerful telescope, they would have surely noticed the telltale fingerprint of retinal in the spectrum of reflected Earth light. But as experienced astronomers, they would have also noticed one fundamental difference – additional absorption lines for nitrogen and magnesium. Those blue and green balls you see at the heart of the chlorophyll molecule." Daniel pointed.

"Oddly different, they probably thought. Where could the extra atoms have come from? With a basic knowledge of chemical bonds, they could have easily reproduced a model of chlorophyll, just as you see here. After that, we can only guess – but these were people who regularly manipulated genetic structures. Could they have seen this new molecule as a manipulation of the original retinal? Molecular engineering? Possibly even the hand of the Designer?"

More murmurs around the arena gave Daniel the reassurance that translations were conveying his story well.

"They were curious. Perhaps fervently. But how could the Ancients get to Earth? By all accounts, they had never developed four-dimensional compression technology. No portals, no instant jump. Colonist history tells us they were a star-faring civilization, but the longest trips were less than thirty light years. The distance to Earth was more than a thousand."

Overhead, Theesah-ma's rotating galactic display still showed the Star Beacon's beam crossing an arm of the galaxy and hitting Earth like a distant bullseye.

"Could they have managed such a distance? First, review what is known. They had genetically engineered their bodies for long interstellar journeys, so they already had expectations that distant worlds were within reach. We also know the Ancients were masters at stellar manipulation. The Star Beacon still operates today, stealing energy from its red dwarf companion. And then, we have the genetic design on the Colonists' backs, a mark that reminds them of the Great Divide."

He had their attention, even the doubters among them. Time to amp it up.

"I'll add one more clue – a small bit of local human knowledge. It's the story of an ordinary star, one among millions. Our astronomers haven't even given it a name just a catalog number, Gliese 710. For years, this star was nothing more than an entry on a list, but then a human astronomer noticed a high radial velocity combined with zero proper motion across the sky. Gliese 710 was coming straight toward us – and fast."

Ajadu and the entire Colonist delegation stood at the edge of their balcony. All eyes were on Daniel.

"As we speak, Gliese 710 is racing toward Earth at fifty-six kilometers per second. It's about sixty light-years away, so we have time before it gets there, but our astronomers are already concerned about the prospects. In a half-million years or so, Gliese 710 could pass close enough to the human solar system to deflect comets in our surrounding Oort Cloud. It could even capture one of our outer planets and drag it away."

A bright star lit up in Theesah-ma's galactic display, labeled Gliese 710. "Perfect timing," Daniel said to Theesah-ma. He wasn't expecting a coordinated presentation or such a convincing graphic.

"Here's the kicker. A few minutes ago, we computed Gliese 710's trajectory. This star is not just heading toward Earth. We traced its path backward. Six million years ago, Gliese 710 was a neighbor of the Star Beacon."

Daniel waved his hand toward the hovering galactic visual with one brightly lit star. "Members of Sagittarius Novus, I give you Dissat, the lost world of the Ancients."

The hush from the audience lasted only seconds before voices began in neighboring balconies and rose to a heated conversation around the arena. The Colonists were particularly animated, talking among themselves and pointing to the star that might represent their lost world.

Nala clapped her approval. It probably would have caught on if anyone else had hands. Sharing her best smile, Nala hugged him. "Nice job."

"Thanks, was I dramatic enough?" He gave a thumbs up to Theesah-ma for her impromptu graphics support.

"Daniel, when you get on a roll, the drama just flows." Her hands made rolling waves in the air to match the sarcasm in her voice.

Daniel laughed, partly in relief that his pitch to a congregation of aliens was over. "And here I thought you loved me."

"Oh, I do. I'll even love the big head you'll have when you're proven right."

"I hope I'm right."

"You are."

A cacophony of voices, none officially translated, made it impossible to gauge audience reaction. Some might claim Daniel's theory was wild speculation, but numbers didn't lie. With Theesahma's help they'd computed quite a few. Gliese 710 was nine degrees offset from the Star Beacon's red laser, precisely the same angle of Earth's drift over six million years. But every good theory needs more than data, it needs a logical story to explain the measurements. The Colonists had supplied one – their story of the Great Divide.

As the ruckus died down, the Colonist diplomat was the first to speak. "An astonishing theory. This star is listed in the An Sath catalog, but as you say, one among millions. Your proposal is not part of our culture. How does a planetary system become a starship?"

Daniel stood up once more. "This might be where a human perspective is advantageous. I've seen how well Jheean engineers manipulate gravity." Daniel pointed to the sphere hovering at Jensen's shoulder. The controlled slide from the top of Bektash's atmosphere was another example. "Around here gravity manipulation seems to be nothing special."

"Fundamental science," one of the avatars on stage said. "It is no different than electricity. Any second-year student could recite the properties of a graviton."

"Maybe so," Daniel said, wondering how many other scientific topics humans might have fallen behind on. "The Ancients may have been proficient too – possibly masters. They've already shown us with the Star Beacon that their engineering was on a stellar scale. Align enough gravitons in the desired direction and you may be able to accelerate a whole star and drag its planets along too. On my own planet, we still wonder how our ancient Egyptian culture built great pyramids, but they did – the pyramids themselves are proof. Likewise, Dissat is proof that a star can be moved."

"But only if it *is* Dissat," another avatar on stage interjected.

"You're right," Daniel admitted. "I can't be sure it's Dissat, but Gliese 710 is not far from Earth. We could easily train our telescopes on its planets. Measure their atmospheric constituents. Check for industrial activity."

The Colonist diplomat interrupted. "We can do better. Your question is easily settled." His avatar pivoted on stage, white robes twirling with a flourish as he addressed the Chitza hedgehog. "I request a remote survey. Send a wedge."

"We accept," the Chitza diplomat replied.

Daniel sat back down and whispered to Jensen. "A wedge?"

"A scout ship," Jensen whispered back. "Wedge shaped. They're used to investigate potentially advanced civilizations. Three years ago, they put one into Earth orbit without us even noticing. Wedges are jet black. Hard to see, and they can hide out in 4-D bubbles – all the stuff your wife knows about."

Nala whispered, "Four-D, sure, but I didn't know about wedges. If they travel via spatial compression, their ship could be at Gliese 710 in the blink of an eye. A great way to verify Daniel's theory."

"Roll call," the Colonist cried out. "On a proposal to send a wedge to the star identified by humans."

The Torak diplomat grumbled, but within seconds Theesah-ma's Milky Way visual was replaced by a three-dimensional floating graphic of a beam balanced on a fulcrum. As voices around the chamber voted, colored beads stacked at one end and the beam tipped until it slid off the fulcrum.

The Colonist on stage announced. "We are agreed. When can Chitza pilots commence?"

"Immediately." The Chitza tapped its communications sphere then disappeared from the stage.

"What's the deal with our little hedgehog friends?" Nala whispered to Secretary Jensen.

Jensen seemed to have all the answers, but then he'd been chained to this process for weeks. "Chitzas operate the wedges. It's one of their contributions to the alliance."

"Those little guys build ships that can jump through 4-D space?"

Jensen nodded. Nala glanced wide-eyed at Daniel, her newfound respect for the spiny balls of cuteness matching his own.

The Sundasti declared an adjournment. Diplomats would move to the antechamber to await results from the wedge. Apparently, Chitza pilots were already warming up their engines.

Like an office at five o'clock, the balconies and glass enclosures quickly cleared out. The four humans shuffled out too, joining with Zin at the balcony entrance.

"What do you think?" Daniel asked Zin.

Zin tipped his head. "Your presentation went well, Dr. Rice. The Colonists and Litian-nolos are clearly on your side, and the remote survey was an excellent idea. I will be very curious to see what the Chitzas find."

"And it may have helped our chances of admission," Secretary Jensen said.

"Yes, I believe it did," Zin answered. "A vote to admit doesn't need to be unanimous, but any dissent would trigger a probationary period followed by an in-depth review. Such a case could last a year or more. The Toraks are on defense but convincing them or their allies not to dissent may require elbow twisting."

"Arm twisting."

"Yes, arm twisting."

Daniel tightened his lips. "Seems like the same situation we've been in for the past three years. We've got the momentum, how do we get this done?" Daniel still had the inflection point in mind. Human admission could ensure those negative futures he had envisioned would be erased. Despite his quirks, Zin had been an outstanding partner as humans learned the ropes of intergalactic affairs. Daniel would hate to say goodbye, as one vision had predicted.

Jensen patted Daniel on the shoulder. "You did your part, Dr. Rice, now it's my turn. I'll mingle in the antechamber and take an informal poll. Can you join me, Zin, for translations?" Zin and Secretary Jensen left together.

Daniel put an arm around Nala. "What'd you think?"

"I want to find out what's out there at Gliese 710."

"Me too."

"But I also think you're the best representative humans could ask for." She squeezed him tight around the waist. "Facts matter. Scientific research matters. Those hidden details? The ones that most people gloss over? They matter. That's how you win."

"We make a good team. If it weren't for you, we wouldn't be here at all. The Death Slide turned out to be a fine choice."

She motioned with a flip of her head. "Come on. I hear they're serving margaritas in the antechamber."

"Really?"

"No, but my cold stare is fierce. They'll figure out the recipe just to get rid of me."

18 WEDGE

DANIEL AND NALA strolled arm in arm through the crowded lobby outside the Council of Equivalence. Glass tubes crisscrossed the open area in a complex dance of intersections, each tube occupied by members bound within their environment.

One tube connected to an aquarium bounded on three sides by glass. The fourth side was open to the air. An impossible vertical wall of water shimmered under bright lights without leaking a drop. Inside, two translucent jellyfish bobbed up and down, their strong central stalks pushing off a sandy floor.

Daniel and Nala exchanged a surprised glance and shouted in unison. "Dancers!"

Ixtlub, the home planet of the underwater species, had been the first off-world expedition for humans two years ago. Since then, humans and Dancers had 'become tight', as one Dancer had quipped, much to the amusement of every human keeping tabs on social media. Daniel's former partner, Marie Kendrick, had been one of the first katanauts to visit the planet. More recently, she'd taken up residence there, and if her social media posts were any indication, was having the time of her life.

Daniel and Nala approached the wall of water, and the two Dancers mirrored their positions only a few feet away. Smaller than a human, the Dancers' translucent white bodies flared to a skirt with multiple tentacles swaying beneath. Their flat eyes were nearly the same translucent white, barely visible near the top of their bell shape. One of the Dancers lifted a tentacle to the tenuous boundary between water and air.

Nala placed her palm opposite the Dancer, and two species touched across the boundary. The Dancer tipped its rounded jellyfish head left and right. Nala smiled. "I've seen so many pictures of them, but it's incredible to be this close. They're so graceful, just like the first video Core sent us."

The second Dancer chirped, its high-pitched voice transferring easily from water to air. "Wee don dotor ice. Imens ohr fens."

Nala exchanged a surprised glance with Daniel. "Was that English? I think it said, well done doctor Rice. Not sure about that last part."

"Humans are friends?" he guessed. They both smiled and the Dancers bobbed in return.

Nala cleared her throat, then eeked at the upper range of her voice. The sound came out something like *syrup* spoken so fast it became one consonant. The Dancers seemed pleased, bobbing left and right in synchronization.

Nala shrugged. "The only Dancer chirp I know."

"Not bad," Daniel said. Though video clips of Dancers and humans interacting were all over the internet back home, only a few human representatives were getting the hang of the Dancer language. The nuances in their peeps and chirps had turned out to be more challenging than most could handle. Even Marie had said she struggled.

Nala brought her left hand up and slid it through the water, with not a drip flowing out. The Dancer lifted a second tentacle and lightly caressed the tips of her fingers. The Dancer's version of a handshake. "You're so soft. Can you understand me?"

There weren't any communication spheres floating nearby. The Dancers produced several more complex sounds but nothing that sounded like English. Not surprising. Even the simple congratulatory statement might have required considerable practice.

Nala stroked the flattened end of the Dancer's tentacle as she'd seen in a how-to-meet-a-Dancer online video. "We've got the physical part down, but there's so much to talk about."

"You're doing just fine." Daniel put his own hand to the undulating water, lightly contacting the Dancer opposite him. "Amazing."

Two Litian-nolos approached from behind. The Dancers withdrew their tentacles, dipped their bells left and right, then pushed off the sandy floor and sped away.

The giants towered overhead, each identical in height and physiology. If not for clothing, trying to figure out who was who might become an embarrassment. Luckily, Theesah-ma's red dress was the distinguishing factor. The giant folded into Nala's embrace.

"TM, you are just incredible," Nala said.

"And your graphics stole the show," Daniel added.

Theesah-ma performed one of her slow-motion blinks. "Pictures are pretty, but words are more powerful. We have just spoken with several members. All were impressed."

"Let's hope I'm right about Dissat." Daniel held out a hand to the other Litian-nolo who wore a blue vest over a silver body suit. "Seishu-kai-do, it's a pleasure to meet you."

The Litian-nolo diplomat's soft head glittered with the same iridescent pinks and violets as Theesah-ma, perhaps a bit more mottled. "Pleased," he cooed, and held out an articulated arm. He brushed the suction-cupped side with Daniel's hand, then did the same with Nala.

Seishu-kai-do's words were halting. "You are as Theesah-ma says. Lovely." He exchanged some cooing sounds with Theesah-ma, then said, "Please forgive. Your language is new. In the antechamber... our tradition..." He seemed unable to complete the sentence, though if

Daniel were challenged to speak a single word of Litian-nolo he'd be hopelessly stumped.

Theesah-ma took over. "Seishu-kai-do wishes to explain that inside the Council of Equivalence, electronic translations ensure no one is misunderstood." She tapped the sphere that hovered at her shoulder. Its lights blinked but the device remained silent. "But here in the antechamber, we communicate with no electronic help. Difficult of course, but pleasurable, too."

Nala leaned in close and whispered something in Theesah-ma's ear that Daniel couldn't make out. Whatever it was, it made the edges of Theesah-ma's head curl.

Before Daniel could ask, a Chitza hedgehog rolled up to their foursome, an impossibly small creature when next to the giant Litian-nolos. Its quills flattened, and its circular body opened to display a white belly. It squeaked repeatedly to Seishu-kai-do who bent lower to listen.

The giant returned to his half-height fold. "My friend explains… their wedge has arrived…"

Theesah-ma finished the rest. "Even now, the wedge scouts for planets around your star, Gliese 710. A report may come in moments."

The hedgehog crossed tiny brown arms over its white belly and made a final squeak to punctuate the certainty of its claim.

"Efficient little guys," Nala said. She squatted and waved fingers to the small creature, who maintained its stoic stance with no more than a ruffle of its quills.

"They are so cute," Nala whispered to Daniel. "That tiny nose just kills me." He nudged her in the ribs to stop but couldn't help smiling at her well-meaning obsession over the adorable furballs.

"How will we know what they find?" Daniel asked.

Seishu-kai-do motioned to the ceiling. There wasn't anything there. "We will all watch."

The room was still crowded with creatures, some standing in the open-air portion of the lobby, but other more exotic figures looming from within their protective tubes. Apparently, everyone knew the procedure. If the Chitzas claimed their wedge had traversed more than a thousand light-years of deep space, no one here doubted it.

Two white-robed figures approached and joined their growing group. With hoods up, only their hawk-like beaks showed, but one lowered his hood to show a wrinkled face and squinty eyes that Daniel was sure he recognized.

"Ajadu."

"Daniel," Ajadu replied, hugging Daniel with bird claws. The sphere hovering at Ajadu's shoulder was quiet as he spoke. "Meh dee wash da tleeg." He motioned a claw to his companion. "Pidanj."

With pride, Daniel remembered the Colonist greeting. "Drangen koolt, Pidanj."

The Colonist diplomat bowed with a flourish of its robes. "Drangen sheeb. Dix nbor."

Nala raised her eyebrows. "Jesus Daniel, you've become an intergalactic linguist, too?" The rest of the group seemed equally impressed. There might be hope for daft humans yet.

Pidanj lowered his hood to reveal a sharper beak and smoother skin than Ajadu – perhaps no more than a youngish two hundred years old.

"I wouldn't be here without this guy," Daniel said to Ajadu and everyone else. "I'm glad we finally reconnected. Apparently, it's about to get interesting."

"It most definitely is," Nala said, pointing to a cylinder-shaped robot that floated in. The bot carried a tray of four glasses, each filled with golden liquid. Nala took two glasses and handed them to Theesah-ma and Seishu-kai-do, and the other two for herself and Daniel.

"Uh, three more please." Nala held up fingers. "For our new friends." The floating cylinder zipped away.

Daniel stared into the glass. Something like ice cubes floated in the gold liquid. He had a sneaking suspicion.

"It's called a margarita," Nala explained to the group. She took a sip. "And I must say the bartender did pretty well."

"How?" Daniel was still perplexed.

Nala winked at Theesah-ma who sipped her own drink. The giant choked slightly, and her green eyes grew wide. "Interesting. Humans have much to offer."

Daniel took his own swig, then hugged his wife – one of a kind. She might be celebrating early, but he'd never fault her for that. Life is short, and Nala was good about acknowledging successes along the way. They'd completed their part in the mystery of the Ancients, the rest was up to others.

Surrounded by such diversity it was hard to step back from the cocktail party atmosphere and reflect on what was at stake. Somewhere in the crowd, Secretary Jensen was shaking hands and making pitches, pushing for a positive outcome for humanity. The Colonists seemed hopeful too. This collection of civilizations might try for equivalence, but not every member was held in equivalent esteem. For some, the two white-robed elders were liars. Even the sweet natured Litian-nolos, Colonists were simpletons mired in quaint folklore.

And meanwhile, a vessel piloted by smart hedgehogs was plying four-dimensional space, searching for a lost race of people who might be Colonist ancestors. Daniel was still getting used to the speed at which the galaxy could be reconnoitered. Rocket launches requiring years to reach a destination were as old fashioned as room-sized computers. Telescopes – even the size of the Star Beacon – were obsolete.

Extra dimensions and spatial compression had always been the key for humans or anyone else. Any civilization that discovered this science opened a door to the universe. But civilizations that never constructed a particle accelerator to pursue what was arguably an obscure – and some would say *useless* science – would remain forever hidden among a sea of stars. The Ancients, for whatever reason, had never made the discovery. It begged the question how many other civilizations might still be out there.

The Chitza raised both tiny arms, squeaking repeatedly. Above their heads, a glowing ball expanded to fill half the antechamber. It formed a planet depicted in three dimensions. Blue oceans were partly obscured by swirls of white clouds. In places, the clouds parted to reveal brown land tinged with the purples of retinal-based plants.

"Is this transmitted live?" Nala asked.

Theesah-ma answered. "Yes, from the wedge. It appears to be a planet orbiting your star, Gliese 710." The Chitza squeaked its agreement.

As they watched, a spacecraft shaped like a slice of pie appeared in the foreground. Black with complex curves, one red light blinked at its tail. The wedge – with its Chitza pilots – descended toward the planet.

The crowd inched closer to the overhead 3-D display transmitted from a thousand light years away. A gleaming metal satellite zipped past, then another from the opposite direction. An alien voice echoed across the lobby, followed by murmurs from the enrapt audience.

"Technology confirmed," Theesah-ma translated. "Intelligent life!"

Nala beamed. Daniel nervously tapped fingers together. So far so good, but a satellite was no guarantee this civilization had survived their six-million-year journey. Anxiety and excitement mixed as real-time discovery played out before their eyes. With the wedge hidden within a bubble of four-dimensional space, it would be impossible to detect by three-dimensional technology. Like a camera gliding toward a flat piece of paper, any citizens living in that flat page would be unaware they were being observed from above.

The wedge descended into a thick atmosphere, piercing a layer of white clouds. Beneath the clouds, a shimmering blue ocean stretched to the horizon with glittering dots scattered haphazardly across the water. Flying lower, the dots resolved to mushroom shapes that perched above the water, each covered with structures of various heights and shapes.

The wedge zoomed past one of the mushroom cities close enough to reveal activity across its surface: rotating wind turbines, aircraft in flight, and traffic along city streets. The alien narrator's voice boomed out over the lobby once more, followed by shouts from the audience.

"Active civilization confirmed," Theesah-ma translated.

Nala pulled on Theesah-ma's arm. "This is great! Is this what all of you were doing when Earth was first discovered?" Both Litian-nolos nodded with a twist of their heads.

Three years ago, Earth would have been the three-dimensional image hovering over the antechamber. Daniel imagined a Chitza-piloted wedge passing over New York or Paris with millions of people below none the wiser. This time, humans were participants in the excitement of discovery – not yet equal among peers, but at least they'd provided exotic drinks for the party.

A new planet with new people. The evidence so far was dramatic, but it would take more than aerial reconnaissance to prove this was the lost planet Dissat from Colonist folklore.

The wedge continued its flight over the ocean, every few seconds passing another mushroom city towering above the waves. Ahead, mountains tinged in purple loomed. The wedge rose slightly, passing over a rugged coastline where waves crashed against a jumble of rocks.

Just beyond, a much larger city filled a valley between mountain peaks. A jumble of buildings large and small cascaded down the mountain slopes and filled central flatlands. Sunlight glinted off shiny surfaces. Skyscrapers soared above the city, their lofty tips almost reaching to a layer of scattered clouds. Elevated tracks carried sleek trains through gaps between the buildings. Gyrocopters navigated the skies.

An enormous arch, thick at its twin bases but thinning at its apex, spanned from one edge of the city to the other. Beneath the arch, a complex tower composed of multicolored bubbles stood taller than most buildings. The collection of bubbles blossomed at its top, looking like an abstract rose growing in the heart of the city.

Nala pointed with a puzzled look on her face, but whatever she'd noticed was left unsaid as the drama continued to unfold.

The black wedge continued its descent toward the roof of one of the taller buildings. A blue circle in the roof's center resolved to a pool of water where dozens of dark-skinned creatures gathered around its perimeter. Some splashed in the water, some observed from the sidelines. None noticed the alien spacecraft, now only meters above them but in an alternate dimension these people knew nothing about.

Each wore an orange cloth that formed a band around their midsection. A large beak – a Colonist's beak – dominated their heads.

Most astonishingly, a bright white line ran down the back of each individual, splitting into a two-pronged fork.

The white-robed Colonist leaped, pointing to the image. "Dix shtinen asa kleeb! Asa kleeb!"

Nala gasped. "It's their genetic mark. It's really them, the Ancients!"

"Holy moly," Daniel said, shaking his head. He clinked glasses with Nala and with the Litian-nolos, then turned to his Colonist friend. "You were right, Ajadu. Your people were right all along." Theesahma stopped guzzling her margarita long enough to help with the translation.

"The mark is proof," Seishu-kai-do said, his gaze turning toward his white-robed companion. "The Colonists and the Ancients are one people."

The Colonist diplomat threw two sticklike arms around Seishu-kaido, then turned to Daniel, bowing. "Jeeg klanik dzer gotzen. Dinken doze."

"He thanks you," Seishu-kai-do said. "And asks if he can touch."

Daniel nodded and reached out with both arms, hugging the bird man. "I'm glad to have helped. But we couldn't have done it without Ajadu."

The floating cylinder returned with another tray of glasses, one miniature in size. "Hey, perfect timing." Nala passed the next round of margaritas to the Colonists and carefully handed a thimble-sized glass to the Chitza, who eagerly accepted it. She lifted a glass. "To the Colonists, whose honor is restored."

Daniel appreciated the success as much as anyone, but his thoughts were one step ahead. "Could I ask a question to our Colonist friends? When Earth was discovered, Core sent a representative, Aastazin, to build Earth's first portal. The portal gave us access to the Dancers and to all of you. Assuming the same thing happens for Dissat, will the Colonists make a visit? Will they reintroduce themselves to their long-lost cousins? Maybe invite the Ancients into the modern world as an honored member of Sagittarius Novus?"

It was a complicated ask, but Seishu-kai-do didn't need translation help from Theesah-ma. "I too have these questions." He spoke with both Colonists at length, the back and forth between Ajadu and the Colonist diplomat making it clear the answer wasn't a simple yes. The alien conversation ended, and Seishu-kai-do held his head low, perhaps surprised, perhaps just thinking.

"Well?" Daniel asked.

Seishu-kai-do lifted his head. "They say no. The Ancients began their journey long ago. They say, let them finish."

19 HOMEWARD

"FINISH THEIR JOURNEY?" Nala echoed. "That's crazy. Dissat won't make it anywhere near Earth for a hundred thousand years. But if somebody builds a portal for them, they could step through to Florida. Or Beijing. We'd be happy to show them around, give them some of our plants, host a scientific lecture on chlorophyll. Hell, we'd throw a worldwide party in their honor."

"The Colonists think it is not wise," Seishu-kai-do repeated.

Daniel rubbed his chin. "I suppose he has a point when you think about it. Six million years ago these people decided to set sail across the galaxy, taking their star and their planet with them. With long lives, their concept of time is quite different than ours. From their perspective, this trip is ninety-five percent complete. Just keep sailing a little longer, and they'll cap off the greatest journey in history."

Nala looked ruffled. "I completely disagree. Someone should tell the people of Dissat they've been discovered. If it were me, I'd want to know. Any scientist would. Daniel, three years ago, while you and I were trying to figure out how to rescue stranded astronauts, the Chitzas sent a wedge to Earth. They saved our astronauts and gave us enough clues to figure out how to meet Core. What if they'd just turned around and gone home? Those astronauts would be dead now, and we'd still have no idea that any of this existed." She waved her arms around the antechamber.

"All good points," Daniel admitted.

Theesah-ma translated Nala's comments for the Colonists. This time Ajadu jumped into the discussion. "Asa klage ni tjab."

Daniel was surprised to hear words he understood. "We left to stay behind. You're right, Ajadu. A phrase that made no sense suddenly has meaning. Since Dissat was the vessel for the journey, Colonists literally had to leave home to stay behind."

"How wonderful. A confusing puzzle solved," Theesah-ma said.

It was tempting to think of Colonists as runaways forsaking their home world while ancient ancestors undertook the greatest feat of engineering ever attempted. But perhaps the Colonists were the more sensible group. There would be dangers in any voyage across the galaxy. Interstellar debris, a stray black hole. Once you've launched your planet against the galaxy's natural rotation, you're swimming upstream.

"I see good points on both sides," Daniel said. "So, who will make the decision about whether to contact them?"

"The Council is responsible," Seishu-kai-do said. "If we agree, Core will initiate contact. If not…"

Daniel finished. "Then Dissat will continue their voyage, blissfully unaware of the larger society all around them. Their own Fermi paradox."

It seemed like a discussion worth having but unlike Earth's case where astronauts were down to their last breaths, the Council had no reason to rush to a decision. What's a year or two when a trip is measured in the millions?

Nala poked Theesah-ma. "I have another idea. Bring up that chlorophyll model you projected back in the council."

Theesah-ma did as Nala asked. A three-dimensional construct of the now famous molecule appeared over their heads. Nala studied it from all sides.

"Thin tail, big head. Less like a rose and more like a sperm if you ask me. But one thing I'm sure of – we all just saw this design in their city. Remember that stack of colored bubbles under the arch? At first,

I thought it might be a sculpture – you know, art on a gigantic scale. But it's more than that. It's a fricken monument."

"A monument? To chlorophyll?" Theesah-ma asked.

Daniel's jaw dropped as he stared at his wife. "You're right! That's exactly what it was. Those colored bubbles were atoms. The Ancients built a molecular monument to chlorophyll right in the middle of their city."

Daniel smiled to Nala. "Nice one."

Nala shrugged. From the astonished looks around them, humans had just earned their place in scientific legend. Along with brainstorming, *connecting the dots* to arrive at a subtle association might forever be described as uniquely human qualities – and maybe they were.

The two Colonists and Seishu-kai-do excused themselves to spread the news to others. Ajadu said a long goodbye to Daniel in untranslated words that somehow still carried meaning. Daniel embraced his new friend. He had not only saved Daniel's life but Ajadu's help may have altered the path for humanity. Perhaps the two would meet again someday and discuss the future over a glass of jurg. Daniel would enjoy that.

The Chitza diplomat stayed put. He even ordered another round of margaritas and when the waiter bot returned, the tray held three thimbles instead of one.

"Hard core partier," Nala whispered. "Going to be a long night for that little guy."

"Yeah, keep this one away from the truly brain damaging stuff."

"Like the TV remote?"

Images of masked singers and slime-covered game show contestants flooded Daniel's head. "Gads, they're going to hate us once they really get to know us."

Nala waved a hand. "Nah, we'll be fine. A few vices, sure, but we've also got Halloween, chocolate chip cookies, and rainbows. Don't forget about our rainbows."

Daniel smiled. Earth and its clever inhabitants could hold their own among this crowd.

A Torak scurried across the floor, rose to an upright position, and slipped between Theesah-ma and Nala. It spread multiple fans of finger-like extensions at the base of its body. A curving pane of dark glass embedded in its helmet seemed to mark where vision organs might be located.

The creature's voice was synthesized but its words came out in English, breaking the antechamber rule for no electronic translations. Toraks were either exempt or didn't care.

"Doctor Daniel Rice. Doctor Nala Pasquier. Welcome."

Though formal, the greeting was already better than anything they'd seen from Toraks in the council chambers. Daniel nodded. Nala stood close, silent.

The electronic voice continued. "I am the Torak representative responsible for inquiries into human qualifications. Though lacking, the human delegation has provided an offsetting proviso, the so-called Theory of Dissat." The helmet lowered its cold stare to the Chitza, who set down its tiny margarita glass, crossed its arms in stoic defiance, and squeaked. The visor returned to Daniel. "*Confirmed* theory."

Daniel did his best to remain cordial. "Glad you see it that way. You'll find that humans can be very resourceful. Possibly on par with our spiny Chitza friends, though it may take us some time to master 4-

D flying wedges as they have done." He waved his hand with a flourish toward the Chitza who squeaked in return.

"Resourceful, perhaps," the Torak helmet pondered. "If aggressive human behavior can be managed…"

"Fine. Help us do that." Daniel crossed his arms to mirror the hedgehog. "We'll help you with your condescension. A win-win."

The Torak adjusted its supporting fans, flicking stiff wires within inches of the tiny Chitza. The Chitza stood its ground. Daniel stood firm too. Even Theesah-ma assumed the crossed-arms stance.

Finally, the Torak spoke. "We shall reconsider our opposition."

Daniel tipped his head. "Great to hear. There's no reason we can't get along. Join us for a drink?"

"Toraks do not drink." The helmet nodded to both Daniel and Nala, then folded the fan back into its body and scurried away.

"How interesting," Theesah-ma said. "I have never seen a Torak back down before. Not even for a trivial mistake."

"Yeah, we have people like that on Earth too," Nala said.

The tiny hedgehog raised its glass and squeaked. Theesah-ma translated. "He says he is proud to stand with humans."

Nala smiled. "You know, I'm really starting to like these guys." She squatted and clinked glass to thimble. The Chitza winked at her though it could have meant almost anything in its native body language.

Within minutes, an announcement came across the antechamber. Theesah-ma explained that all diplomats were being recalled to the council chambers to vote.

The Chitza chugged the rest of his margarita, bowed to Daniel and Nala, then hopped away into a growing stream of diplomats heading toward the council chamber, including Secretary Jensen who waved as he hurried by.

As the crowd thinned, Zin appeared with an s-bot trailing close behind. As they approached, Daniel studied the mechanical grasshopper, its features familiar but shinier. "It can't be, can it?"

Zin's eyes flicked in excited animation. "It is, Dr. Rice. Fully repaired and restored to working condition. I supervised the rehabilitation myself."

Daniel lowered, fixing on the dark glassy eyes, now polished to perfection. "Tozz, is it really you?"

The voice was pitched in a higher octave. "Three one zero zero. Hero of the Bektash desert."

Nala broke into peals of laughter. "Damn straight you're a hero."

"Torak rejected. Electrocution not protocol. Order restored."

It was the longest string of words Daniel had heard from the bot. It seemed positively pleased with itself. Nala leaned close and gave Tozz a kiss on its polished head. "Thank you for saving Daniel."

Tozz recoiled from the not-protocol kiss, then with a twitch, recovered its composure. "Human alive. Good."

Daniel was enjoying the show. He gave the bot a pat. "Nice work, Tozz, you've got it all figured out. How'd they put you back together? When I left, you were in pretty bad shape."

"Restoration protocol," Tozz squeaked, as proud as any college graduate.

Zin elaborated. "Its head is a replacement, but the engineers did a full memory restore from an upload sent just before the bot self-destructed. Once powered up, the engineers could hardly finish their system test. Three one zero zero kept asking about you, Dr. Rice."

"Aw, that's sweet," Nala said.

Daniel wasn't about to let the bot's moment of pride slip away. "Tozz, if you're not busy with other service requests, Nala and I could use your protection to make sure we get home safely."

"Accepted," Tozz answered. The bot scooted closer to Daniel and raised on its haunches.

For the next ten minutes, Tozz didn't move from its guardian position while Zin explained what was likely going on inside the council chambers. There might be more than one vote, both for human membership but also for the Torak case. The whole matter could be referred to Core for investigation, followed by discipline or rehabilitation – of a sentient kind.

"Galactic justice. It has some logic to it," Daniel said. Core was no doubt up to the task.

Minutes later, the stream of diplomats reversed direction, with Secretary Jensen one of the first out. His smile told the story. "It's done! We're in!"

The three humans embraced. "Fabulous news. You did a great job, Nikolaus."

"Your presentation was the turning point, Daniel. Everyone loves a good story, and there's not a single species who doesn't know the history of the Ancients. For them, it's like Tutankhamun's tomb. Everyone is still stirred up over the discovery of Dissat."

Zin was just as excited. "Your chlorophyll theory seems to have hit the needle on the head, Dr. Rice."

"Nail. Nail on the head." Daniel waved him off. "Never mind."

Nala hooked into Jensen's arm, "Mr. Secretary, will you be our first representative to Jheean?"

"Are you offering, Dr. Pasquier?"

"I am. On behalf of the other eight billion back home, you're our man."

Jensen looked around. A mystifying variety of species strolled through the antechamber with still more occupying a confusion of tubes running up, down, left, and right. "Jheean is more complicated than the UN, but I could get used to it." He tapped Zin. "Which reminds me, we need to get back to Earth and let everyone know."

Zin motioned with his arm toward the exit. "First Ambassador Jensen, the portal is waiting."

Astonishingly, they could be back in Florida or Beijing before dinner. Nala gave Zin a quick hug and promised they'd be right behind. There was one final goodbye to take care of.

Through a shower of congratulations from the crowd, Jensen and Zin departed for Earth. There was no question the man would return as Earth's first ambassador to Sagittarius Novus, and no question that he'd fit in well with this diverse collection of diplomats.

Theesah-ma caressed Nala's hair with a suckered hand. "Must you go?"

Nala returned the touch. "Hey, we don't even have security passes anymore. You blasted them into a star." So far, Tozz wasn't making any bones about their brazen act of trespassing. "But we're not going anywhere until we fix Daniel's head."

When Nala latched onto something, she never let go, a single-minded focus that Daniel appreciated about his wife. Unfortunately, Theesah-ma had never made any promise to *fix* his mental entanglement. Since the episode at the underwater portal, he hadn't had any further memories of alternate futures, but that didn't mean they wouldn't come once more.

Theesah-ma joined hands with Daniel and Nala. Her voice was soft. "Lovely Daniel, my time traveling friend. Alas, entanglement is permanent. You do not wish to hear this. I understand. But good can result from your condition. When convenient for you both, please come to my home. I will show you."

Nala asked, "Come to your planet? Can we do that?"

"You are members now, with full rights of portal travel. Your Zin can make the arrangements. When you come, I will take Daniel to our time mentor's hospital."

Daniel squinted. "Wait… a hospital?"

"Perhaps more like a resort. A place where time mentors confer with one another. They will welcome you, I am sure. After all, you are entangled not just with yourself but with them too."

Daniel would be more than happy to learn how to prevent more of the disturbing dreams even if it required going to an alien hospital. "I'd like that… I think. I already feel better just knowing that temporal entanglement is a *thing*. At least, I'm not crazy. Of course, it might get weird again if another inflection point comes along. That could happen, right?"

"Yes, it could. It probably will. You may even instigate one without intention. Today you are untrained. You see confusing visions with no sense of control. A trained time mentor sees probability pathways and makes reasoned choices. There is a difference."

Daniel took a deep breath. There didn't seem to be any way to avoid it. He might be forever tied to future memories. They might come like uninvited guests when he least expected it.

Nala noticed his reticence. She always did.

She put a hand on his shoulder, her voice almost as soft as Theesah-ma's. "Daniel, you always say you want a simple life. You left your White House job. Moved to Santa Fe with me. And, yeah, we got some of that simpler life. Sipping wine on the patio. Hikes in the mountains. Sunday mornings in bed, just you and me. Great stuff."

Nala scrunched up her face in that cute way she had when tougher words were coming. "But... simpler doesn't mean you have to be a recluse, or a worrier, or... a Death Slide weenie." She smiled at the last part. "That's not who you are. You're the great Daniel Rice. The guy who finds evidence others miss. The guy who makes sense of this weird world. Sure, you didn't ask for this entanglement stuff, but here it is. Maybe you should... I don't know... embrace it? Label it as the extraordinary part of you. Your superpower. TM is offering a way to manage it. And I'm offering unwavering support, no matter what happens, and no matter where any of these *future memories* take you."

Daniel pulled her close and kissed her. "You're right. I guess I was being... um..."

"A weenie?"

He smiled. "Too preoccupied with the idea that I had to ditch the limelight and the bigshot White House job... so I could have you."

"Daniel, you've got me. It's not one or the other."

"Yeah, I see that." He kissed her again, much to Theesah-ma's interest. "Alright, if I'm going to be humanity's time mentor, I guess I'll need some training. Theesah-ma, I accept your invitation. If your Jheean apartment is any indication, I'm sure your planet is beautiful."

"It is," Theesah-ma said. "I shall so enjoy showing it to you." The giant touched a suckered hand to Daniel's lips and then to Nala's. "Do that again."

They looked askance at each other, then kissed once more.

"Fascinating. This connection between you involves no food transfer?"

Nala doubled over in laughter. "Holy bejesus, TM, you've *got* to come to our planet. What a hoot that would be. Kissing is just a warmup." Still laughing, Nala wrapped arms around Theesah-ma, an act that took some effort given their size difference. Nala had made a lifelong friend. Parting wouldn't be easy even with a promise to get together again.

Daniel echoed the impromptu invitation. "Please do. Come visit us. Stay with us at our house in Santa Fe. There might be a few logistical issues, but I'm sure we could work it out."

"Such as the gravity?" Theesah-ma stretched her jointed legs.

Nala waved both hands. "It's not that bad, just a little stronger than here. Plus, we have a swimming pool at our house. In the water you'll feel weightless."

Theesah-ma's head curled. "Then I will come. I will visit my new human friends on their unusual green planet. And I will swim in their pool."

Three friends tangled in a final group hug. Then, with lots of waves and air kisses, Daniel and Nala departed for their journey home.

Tozz guided them through the maze of tubes, finally exiting through the King-Kong-sized black wall and into the grand avenue of Jheean's oxygen petal.

Light ovals blinked at the avenue's edge. They hopped on with Tozz leaping beside them, never straying more than a few yards from Daniel. This time their passage was without stops. They zipped by markets, cross streets, and the variety of member species, each physical form now more familiar.

At the corridor's end, they hopped off at the domed landing zone where they had alighted earlier in the day. Tozz issued a high-pitched squeal, and a slit opened in the glass barrier.

"I think we can take it from here, buddy," Daniel told the grasshopper bot.

Tozz stood on its haunches, its black glassy eyes still showing no hint of the significant intelligence beneath.

Nala contorted with a sad frown. "It's like leaving a faithful dog behind." She lifted Tozz's chin. "What a sweetheart you are under that metal skin."

Tozz sniffed. "Humans. Kind."

"We try," Daniel said. "You take care of yourself. No more self-destructing, okay? That stuff is not protocol."

Tozz twitched its head. "Service requested."

"Somebody else calling you?"

"Yes." Tozz looked up. "Goodbye Daniel Rice."

The s-bot leaped away to fulfill whatever duty it had been asked to perform. Daniel watched as the bot disappeared around a corner, then wiped watery eyes. He hooked arms with Nala, and they passed together into the departure platform.

A gold capsule hovered a foot above the floor. They took seats, its door closed, and the capsule began a gentle ascent into the vertical tube stretching above.

Now late in the Bektash day, a red sun sank to the horizon and lit scattered clouds with varying shades of orange and pink. Lights outlined the edge of the Jheean megastructure that sprawled across darkening hues of the desert.

"Amazing place," Nala said as the capsule accelerated upward.

"It was. Amazing people, too. Bots included."

"Let's come back."

"A great place to mingle, that's for sure. Twenty-three species."

"Twenty-four now. Maybe twenty-five, if we include the Ancients."

The capsule shot upward toward a darkening sky. Stars began to show themselves, including a sparkling glass cocoon that caught the last rays of the sun.

Daniel mused. "We can't just leave the Ancients hanging out there all alone. With portal technology and the Chitza's wedge ship, it would be easy to pop over to Dissat. Tell them about humans and Earth. Fill them in on how their cousins the Colonists are doing. How much fun would that be?"

Nala leaned in close, snuggling. "When I lived in Chicago, I always loved it when friends visited. It's a nice feeling to show people stuff they've never seen before. Rewarding. I think it's why Theesah-ma liked being with us."

"Hmm, human centric. We have to be careful about assigning our emotions to other species."

"Oh, I don't know. I think we have a lot in common. Litian-nolos for sure. Colonists too. Even the Chitzas – god I want to take one of them home. So cute."

Daniel glared. Nala glared back, then flashed her most playful grin. No further words were required. Regardless of how advanced their species had proven to be, in Nala's mind the Chitza hedgehogs would always be cute.

The glass cocoon above grew larger by the second. Now near the top of the Bektash atmosphere, the Milky Way spread across the sky. Nala craned her neck. "Isn't that Theesah-ma's star cluster? We're definitely going there, just as soon as Zin can arrange it."

Daniel nodded his agreement. "Every mentor deserves a trip to the mentor hospital." He scrunched his nose. "What a terrible name."

"Daniel, it's not a *mental* hospital. It's just specialized for you bad ass time travelers. Besides, Theesah-ma said it was like a resort. They probably have a golf course."

"She was pretty good at sales pitches."

"Hey, the Star Beacon lived up to the hype."

"It did," Daniel admitted.

Nala was quiet for a minute as the capsule slowed. "I like her a lot."

"Me too."

Once home, Daniel would get the gears turning to make the Litian-nolo trip a reality. They'd need more than just Zin's help; it would probably require high-level approvals. After all, they'd be the first human visitors. But Daniel had plenty of contacts; he'd make it happen, and not just to manage his entanglement. He'd do it for Nala. She made friends easily, but Theesah-ma was in a new category.

The capsule slid into place beneath the lofty glass cocoon. Inside, two transfer seats waited on the platform. No Zin. No Secretary Jensen. They'd already departed. No matter, the transfer chairs were capable of automated return.

Daniel strapped in to one seat, Nala in the other. They held hands across the gap.

Nala blew a kiss. "You did well, lovely Daniel."

He laughed. "You too, lovely Nala. Ready?"

With a press of the reset button, hoods came down and their seats slid toward the open portal. Toward Beijing, or maybe Florida. It didn't really matter. Daniel and Nala were heading home.

THE END

AFTERWORD

I hope you enjoyed this story. I had fun writing it. This book is shorter than the previous books in the series with a lower dose of quantum physics. No reason, that's just how it turned out.

I wasn't even planning a fourth book. When I finished *Quantum Time*, I figured three was enough. But then I started thinking about how the craziness of the first three stories would have affected the characters. I worried for Daniel, wondered about Nala. I became a voyeur and peered into their personal lives.

All the while, I received email from readers asking for a story about Core or the alien civilizations introduced in the first three books – a sort of second contact story (if such a category exists). And so, between my voyeurism and your insistence, *Quantum Entangled* was born.

Yes, it's part mystery but the story still has a basis in science – I reached out to chemistry this time. Did you know that both retinal and chlorophyll create a nucleotide called adenosine triphosphate or ATP, a complex organic molecule found in all life on Earth? I didn't. ATP, it turns out, powers life by providing energy needed at the cellular level. It's like the cell's battery.

Discovering how the world works is like my religion, but far more satisfying since it's observed reality. I am continually awed by what evolution can do (and has done). I'm amazed at how complex chlorophyll's chemical reactions can be. And DNA? Don't get me started. How the hell did such a complex, self-replicating molecule emerge from Earth's early chemical soup? Seems like a glorious fantasy, yet that's what really happened. (Read Richard Dawkins's *The Greatest Show on Earth* if you want that same sense of awe but with detailed explanations from a competent biologist).

Chlorophyll is superior to retinal, let's get that straight. Chlorophyll efficiently pulls atoms of carbon directly from the air and makes those atoms available for roots, stems, and branches. That oak table in your dining room was once carbon dioxide molecules floating through the air. Chlorophyll pulled them together into wood.

But retinal almost certainly came first. Why? Because it absorbs green light, and green is the position in the sunlight spectrum where peak radiation occurs. Botanists had always wondered why chlorophyll absorbed in the red and blue, but not in the green. Why would a molecule evolve that doesn't take advantage of most of the sun's energy?

The answer came in 2006 from a scientific paper known as the Purple Earth Hypothesis. The author, microbiologist Shil Dassarma, suggested that retinal had been dominant in Earth's early years (billions of years ago). Back in those days, retinal was widespread, absorbing sunlight in the green peak of the spectrum. Take away green light and you're left with red and blue, which makes purple. Thus, life in those days reflected purple. Our oceans were probably tinted purple from all the single-celled organisms swimming around.

Chlorophyll probably evolved as a competitor, consuming the red and blue light that retinal didn't absorb – the leftovers, so to speak. Once chlorophyll arrived on the scene, retinal's dominance was over. Chlorophyll could create sturdy plants which gave it a huge advantage, especially for colonizing the land. As the years clicked by, chlorophyll won this epic battle. Earth became green, not purple.

It might have gone another way. Chlorophyll might not have evolved at all on Earth. That idea sparked the science in this story. What if chlorophyll's emergence was a rare event? What if most planets took a different path? (*What if...* is usually how I start my plot planning).

If you're curious, here's what a chlorophyll molecule looks like:

Those buds marked H_3C or CH_3 are methyls. Retinal has them too, in much the same structure. The big difference is the central "head" of this sperm-like molecule: four nitrogen atoms surrounding a single magnesium atom. It's called a porphyrin and this structure appears multiple times in organic chemistry. Hemoglobin – the protein in our blood that carries oxygen to the cells – is another porphyrin, except in hemoglobin the magnesium atom is replaced by iron.

See all those O's scattered around? That's oxygen. During plant chemistry, chlorophyll releases it to the air. Ahh. We have something good to breathe. Thank you, chlorophyll. Later, the hemoglobin in our blood carries those same oxygen atoms to our cells using its own porphyrin structure. Same structure serving two different purposes. Isn't chemistry amazing?

Chlorophyll comes in a few different forms, which is strong evidence for biosynthesis (a fancy word for a non-living molecule that adjusts to meet the needs of a living host who is evolving by natural selection). Here's an absorption chart for two of the most common forms of chlorophyll, a and b:

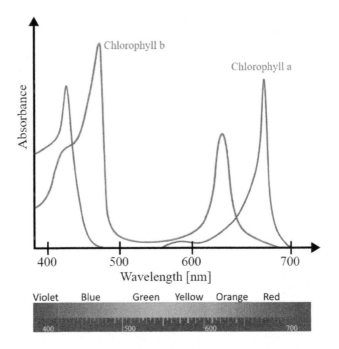

It's easy to see why scientists say chlorophyll absorbs blue and red – the graph shows two very distinct peaks of absorption. And look at the green part of the spectrum. Absorption is near zero, showing that virtually all of the green light is reflected. Voila, we see green plants.

I love chlorophyll. It's physics, chemistry, and biology all wrapped up in a single molecule.

There's another bit of science in this story: Gliese 710. Yes, it's a real star (located near Altair, north of Sagittarius) and it really is heading straight for us at high speed! Beware, our descendants might be in trouble when it gets here.

Allow me to explain further. *Radial velocity* is the motion of a star toward or away from the observer, easily determined by examining the red or blue shift of starlight spectra. *Proper motion* is simply the movement across the sky over time, conceptually easy, but harder to measure since stars move so little in a human lifetime. Light from Gliese 710 is strongly shifted toward the blue – meaning this star is coming toward us – and fast. But its proper motion is close to zero. It's like staring at a bullet coming straight at your forehead.

We might lose a planet or two when Gliese 710 comes flying by. So long, Pluto! Bye Neptune! It was nice knowing you. But I wonder. Could we gain a planet from the encounter? If that happens, we should name it Dissat.

Finally, there are lots of aliens in this story, which was the most fun for me. Ever since childhood, I've tried to imagine realistic aliens. I always hated the bulging head, bug-eyed creatures featured in the

201

comic books I read. Or the humans with pointy ears on TV (sorry Spock). Ideas that aliens might eat us or suck our blood were utterly ridiculous. Two species from entirely different evolutions would have no dependencies on one another. Aliens will not only *not* look like us, if they tried to consume us, they'd no doubt become very ill.

So, what would intelligent beings look like? That's where the fun comes in. Think about all of the physical influences upon Earth life: gravity (life would need to adapt to both stronger and weaker gravities), atmosphere (our own solar system shows a great variety), oceans, temperature variations, seasons (due to a planet's rotational tilt), magnetic field, and on and on. While Earth's specific influences (and the randomness built into evolution) guarantee that Earth life will be unique, that doesn't mean alien life couldn't resemble Earth life in key ways.

For example, eyes have evolved multiple times in Earth's history. They're useful for survival, so it's reasonable to expect eyes (or some kind of photoreceptor) to exist on alien bodies too. On Earth, language, and the organs and brainpower to produce it, is widespread. Though we humans are certainly the champs when it comes to intraspecies communication, dolphins and whales also use voice-based languages. Dogs and cats use a combination of voice and body stance to transmit messages to friends or enemies. Even bees dance to tell their buddies where the flowers are located!

With all this communicating on our own planet, it's not hard to imagine alien language, even if it's based on the complex motions of some body part that we don't even recognize. In Chapter 5, the Virgons twirled pointy appendages to produce vibrations in the air.

There are a hundred other ways in which living organisms might evolve. Aliens could be fundamentally different than anything we've seen – like the Szitzojoots in Chapter 3, a buzzing hive. Or they might remind us of an Earth species – like the Chitzas in Chapter 16, who resemble hedgehogs. I came up with a few alien forms for this story. You might think of more.

For this story, I admit to one significant compromise: intellectual temperament. My aliens all think and behave "logically" – that is, like we humans do. They greet newcomers, show curiosity about new ideas, agree upon rules, and demonstrate emotions like pride, hate, or jealousy. There are good story reasons to restrict the aliens to these boundaries, but there's no evolutionary reason. An alien intelligence might use thought processes so foreign we are forever unfit to comprehend why they behave the way they do, or what they're trying to tell us. So, while an incomprehensible alien intellect might be realistic, it makes for difficult storytelling! Not this time. Maybe I'll tackle that in another book.

****

I'd love to stay in touch (Amazon doesn't give authors information about readers). Please go to http://douglasphillipsbooks.com and add your name to my email list. I'll keep you informed about upcoming books, and I promise I won't fill your inbox with junk. Also, at my website are pictures related to the stories and color versions of each book illustration.

I hoped you enjoyed this fourth book in the Quantum Series. If you did, please consider writing a short review. It doesn't matter if there are already a thousand reviews, yours will be unique, and future readers pay more attention to the most recent reviews anyway. For information on how to leave a review, go to http://douglasphillipsbooks.com/contact.

Afterword

Thanks for reading!

Douglas Phillips

ACKNOWLEDGMENTS

For me, writing is a pleasurable task, but that's not to say it's easy (this book took three rewrites). So many people helped along the way. Thanks to my fellow authors at Critique Circle, but especially Kathryn Hoff, Glenn Frank, Jim Sheasby, Ophélie Quillier, and Maddy Loveridge. It's so nice to bounce ideas off talented people who are writing their own stories. This story is better for your contributions.

Thanks to Rena Hoberman for another beautiful cover. Every cover in this series shares the same style and colors, and I've always loved the brilliant point of light that Rena placed somewhere in each design.

Editing and proof reading are laborious processes, and I'm indebted to Terry Grindstaff for this book (as well as the others in this series). Even after publication, he found typos that nobody else noticed or wording that wasn't kosher. Thank you once more.

Thanks also to ten beta readers who gave me a first indication of how this somewhat different story would be received. Thank you Nancy Bisson, Bill Gill, Ophélie Quillier, Joe Ziber, Lisa Manuel, Lili Vandulek, Craig Crawford, Kelli Wolfe, and Jay Moskowitz for your time and help.

I keep telling my wife, "Just one more book." Writing consumes at least half of my day, every day, which doesn't leave much time for long walks along the beach (or whatever couples are supposed to do). Maybe after this book is published, we'll find a grassy hill, lie on our backs, and gaze up at puffy clouds floating by. That's romantic, right? (But more likely, we'll order Chinese takeout and watch an episode of All Creatures Great and Small – same idea.)

ABOUT THE AUTHOR

Douglas Phillips is the best-selling author of the Quantum Series, a trilogy of science fiction thrillers set in the fascinating world of particle physics where bizarre is an everyday thing. In each story, the pace is quick and the protagonists—along with the reader—are drawn deeper into mysteries that require intellect, not bullets, to resolve.

Douglas has two science degrees, has designed and written predictive computer models, reads physics books for fun and peers into deep space through the eyepiece of his backyard telescope.

The Quantum Series

Quantum Incident (Prologue)

The long-sought Higgs boson has been discovered at the Large Hadron Collider in Geneva. Scientists rejoice in the confirmation of quantum theory, but a reporter attending the press conference believes they may be hiding something.

Nala Pasquier is a particle physicist at Fermi National Laboratory in Illinois. Building on the 2012 discovery, she has produced a working prototype with capabilities that are nothing less than astonishing.

Daniel Rice is a government science investigator with a knack for uncovering the details that others miss. But when he's assigned to investigate a UFO over Nevada, he'll need more than scientific skills. He'll need every bit of patience he can muster.

Quantum Space (Book 1)

High above the windswept plains of Kazakhstan, three astronauts on board a Russian Soyuz capsule begin their reentry. A strange shimmer in the atmosphere, a blinding flash of light, and the capsule vanishes in a blink as though it never existed.

On the ground, evidence points to a catastrophic failure, but a communications facility halfway around the world picks up a transmission that could be one of the astronauts. Tragedy averted, or merely delayed? A classified government project on the cutting edge of particle physics holds the clues, and with lives on the line, there is little time to waste.

Daniel Rice is a government science investigator. Marie Kendrick is a NASA operations analyst. Together, they must track down the cause of the most bizarre event in the history of human spaceflight. They draw on scientific strengths as they plunge into the strange world of quantum physics, with impacts not only to the missing astronauts, but to the entire human race.

Quantum Void (Book 2)

Particle physics was always an unlikely path to the stars, but with the discovery that space could be compressed, the entire galaxy had come within reach. The technology was astonishing, yet nothing compared to what humans encountered four thousand light years from home. Now, with an invitation from a mysterious gatekeeper, the people of Earth must decide if they're ready to participate in the galactic conversation.

The world anxiously watches as a team of four katanauts, suit up to visit an alien civilization. What they learn on a watery planet hundreds of light years away could catapult human comprehension of the natural world to new heights. But one team member must overcome crippling fear to cope with an alien gift she barely understands.

Back at Fermilab, strange instabilities are beginning to show up in experiments, leading physicists to wonder if they ever really had control over the quantum dimensions of space.

Quantum Time (Book 3)

A dying man stumbles into a police station and collapses. In his fist is a mysterious coin with strange markings. He tells the police he's from the future, and when they uncover the coin's hidden message, they're inclined to believe him.

Daniel Rice never asked for fame but his key role in Earth's first contact with an alien civilization thrust him into a social arena where any crackpot might take aim. When the FBI arrives at his door and predictions of the future start coming true, Daniel is dragged into a mission to save the world from nuclear holocaust. To succeed, he'll need to exploit cobbled-together alien technology to peer into a world thirty years beyond his own.

Quantum Entangled (Book 4)

Daniel Rice hasn't felt right since his return from a dystopian future now extinguished. Curious dreams repeat with detailed precision. A voice – or something – seems to be calling him. His problem isn't medical, it's not even scientific, and it's driving his wife crazy.

Nala is worried, and she's not the type to pace the halls while her overly analytic hubby procrastinates. Earth's scientific power couple is soon halfway around the world to consult with alien android, Aastazin. Zin is no doctor, but he has friends in high places. Very high.

Next stop, a thousand light years from home where an alien megacity shaped in a six-petaled flower hosts species from dozens of

209

worlds. An inexplicable attack leaves Daniel wandering across an inhospitable planet and Nala alone among a confusing mashup of sentient beings. With little hope of finding each other, they learn there is more going on at this alien gathering place than they knew – aggressive security bots, an ancient mystery, and a pending vote that could shun humanity from the greatest collection of civilizations the galaxy has ever known.

In book #4 of the series, Daniel and Nala will need to make friends, avoid enemies, and leverage newfound knowledge to reconnect with each other and boost humanity's chance of galactic membership.

Other Books

Phenomena

Amelia Charron is a neuroscientist researching brain disorders. She routinely uses astonishing mind-linking technology that allows her to enter the dream world of patients. Each night, Amelia acts as a guide through the bizarre wonderland of the mind – an assisted lucid dream. It's a technique that reroutes neural pathways to heal the brain, but it's not without psychological dangers for both the patient and the guide.

Orlando Kwon will do anything to keep the frightening voices at bay. Alien voices, he's sure, but he has no idea what they are saying. The medical diagnosis: early-stage schizophrenia. With his life in tatters, a referral to a specialized neuroscience team might be his last chance.

Amelia is startled by what she sees in her newest patient's mind. Frightening dreams of an unknown world are accompanied by knowledge the man couldn't possibly have invented and a language no one has heard. In a race against time, Amelia must uncover the deep implications for her patient, herself, and humankind – before Orlando inserts the final component into a strange device he feels compelled to construct.

Phenomena is a story of intrigue, psychological distress, and one scientist's quest to untangle the mysteries of human consciousness.

MarsBots

NASA and other space agencies were the first to land on Mars, but Earth's billionaires now have their own plans. By the 2030's private exploration dominates – self-funded, unconstrained, profit-motivated.

In this hard science fiction short story, remote-controlled surface rovers are open to the public. Anyone can do it. Just create an account, provide a credit card, then guide your very own "hopper" anywhere you want. Check out the canyons, pose for a selfie with an historic rover, or just kick up some dust as your hopper leaps across the Martian surface at high speed.

But unconstrained exploration by the masses poses new issues that governments are remiss in addressing. Shadowy organizations step in to fill the void, creating new conflicts that play out a world away.

Printed in Great Britain
by Amazon